The walls trembled and shook with automatic fire. Rebecca spun and trained her weapon on the back door, her heart pounding in her throat. The disbelief and terror in Steve's voice made her blood run cold.

—zombies?

She shot a glance back, saw Steve still shooting at something, saw David motioning her to move.

She sidled for the open door, catching a sickening, up-close look at the bullet-riddled corpse still hanging there. The head had caved in like a rotting pumpkin, teeth shattered, gummy flecks of tissue radiating out from behind the skull. The waving hand was no longer connected to the rotting arm, the radius and ulna blown away. It dangled there like some obscene decoration, beckoning . . .

Steve fired once more and the auto's clatter ceased. He raised the weapon, his eyes wide with shock as he opened his mouth to say something—

—and the back door crashed open, bullets flying through the dark in a blaze of orange fire. David pushed her roughly through the front and she ran, the responding *crack* of nine-millimeter rounds resonating behind her.

Turning, she saw Karen firing, heard John yelling, "Come on, come *on*—"

It seemed that Umbrella had found a new application for the T-Virus. *And like it or not,* Rebecca thought, *we're going to have to deal with the consequences.*

They were trapped in Caliban Cove. And in this facility, the creatures had guns.

RESIDENT EVIL

CALIBAN COVE

S.D. PERRY

POCKET BOOKS
New York   London   Toronto   Sydney   Tokyo   Singapore

This book is a work of fiction. Names, characters, places and incidents are products of the author's imagination or are used fictitiously. Any resemblance to actual events or locales or persons, living or dead, is entirely coincidental.

An *Original* Publication of POCKET BOOKS

POCKET BOOKS, a division of Simon & Schuster Inc.
1230 Avenue of the Americas, New York, NY 10020

ISBN: 0-671-02440-X

First Pocket Books printing October 1998

10 9 8 7 6 5 4 3 2 1

POCKET and colophon are registered trademarks of Simon & Schuster Inc.

Cover art by Gerber Studio

Printed in the U.S.A.

For Leslie, hole-digger extraordinaire.

"Through avarice, evil smiles; through insanity, it sings."

—Anonymous

CALIBAN COVE

PROLOGUE

Raccoon Times, July 24, 1998

SPENCER MANSION DESTROYED IN EXPLOSIVE FIRE

RACCOON CITY—At approximately 2 A.M. Thursday morning, Victory Lake district residents were awakened by an explosive blast that thundered through northwest Raccoon Forest, apparently caused by a fire that swept through the abandoned Spencer mansion and ignited chemicals stored in the basement. Due to delays from the police barricade set up at the forest perimeter (in connection with the recent string of murders in Raccoon City), local firefighters were unable to salvage any part of the estate's grounds. After a three-hour battle against the raging fire, the thirty-one-year-old mansion and adjacent servant's quarters were deemed a complete loss.

Built by Lord Oswell Spencer, European aristocrat and one of the founders of the worldwide pharmaceutical company, Umbrella, Inc., the estate was designed by award-winning architect George Trevor as a guest house for Umbrella VIPs and was closed down shortly after completion for reasons unknown. According to Amanda Whitney, spokesperson for the Umbrella Corporation, parts of the estate were still being used to store a number of industrial cleaning agents and solvents used by Umbrella. Whitney said in a statement yesterday that the company would take full responsibility for the unfortunate incident, calling it "a serious oversight on our part. Those chemicals should have been cleared out of the Spencer house a long time ago, and we're just thankful that no one was hurt."

At this point, the cause of the fire is undetermined, but Whitney went on to say that Umbrella will be bringing in their own investigators to sift through the ruins in hopes of determining the fire's point of origin. . . .

Raccoon Weekly, July 29, 1998

S.T.A.R.S. TAKEN OFF MURDER INVESTIGATION

RACCOON CITY—In a surprising announcement by city officials at a press conference yesterday, the Raccoon City branch of the Special Tactics and Rescue Squad (S.T.A.R.S.) was officially removed from the investigation into the nine brutal murders and five disappearances of city residents that have occurred in the last ten weeks. City council member Edward Weist delivered the statement, citing gross incompetence as the primary reason for the S.T.A.R.S. removal.

Readers may remember that the S.T.A.R.S.'s first action upon being assigned the cases last week was to search the northwest area of the forest for the alleged cannibal killers. Weist stated that it was because of their "blatantly unprofessional conduct" that their mission ended in disaster, resulting in the crash of a helicopter and the loss of six of their eleven team members, including the S.T.A.R.S. branch commander, Captain Albert Wesker.

"After [the S.T.A.R.S.'s] mishandling of the Raccoon Forest search," said Weist, "we've decided to let the RPD see this investigation through to its conclusion. We have reason to believe that the S.T.A.R.S. may have been ingesting drugs and/or alcohol prior to their search, and have suspended the use of their services indefinitely."

Weist was joined by Sarah Jacobsen (representing Mayor Harris) and Police Commissioner J.C. Washington to make the announcement and answer questions. Neither Police Chief Brian Irons nor any of the surviving S.T.A.R.S. could be reached for comment. . . .

Cityside, August 3, 1998

SOURCE OF ESTATE FIRE DEEMED ACCIDENTAL

RACCOON CITY—After an exhaustive investigation by fire officials working with Umbrella, Inc.'s ISD (Industrial Services Division), the fire that ravaged the company-owned Spencer estate in Raccoon Forest late last month was determined to have been caused by carelessness on the part of person or persons unknown, as was announced in a press conference yesterday. Said ISD Team Leader David Bischoff, "It looks like somebody tried to start a campfire in one of the mansion's rooms and things just got out of control. We've found nothing to suggest arson or foul play of any kind." He went on to say that while the destruction of the property was total, there's no evidence that anyone was caught in the fire or subsequent explosion.

Chief Brian Irons of the Raccoon City Police Department was in attendance at the conference, and when asked whether he believed the fire to be connected to the unsolved murders and disappearances plaguing the city, Irons stated that there was no way to be sure. Said Irons, "At this point, anything I could say would only be speculation—though I will say that the fact that the murders have stopped since the night of the fire seems to imply that perhaps the killers were hiding there. We can only hope that they've now left the area and will soon be apprehended."

Chief Irons refused to comment on the allegations of gross misconduct by the S.T.A.R.S. in their brief assignment to the murder investigation, saying only that he agreed with the city council's decision and disciplinary actions are being considered. . . .

Oɴᴇ

REBECCA CHAMBERS RODE HER MOUNTAIN
bike through the dark, winding streets of the Cider
district, the late summer moon swelling in the warm,
clear night sky overhead. Although it was relatively
early, the suburban streets were deserted, the citywide
curfew still in effect; no one under eighteen was
supposed to be out after dusk until the murderers
were caught and put safely behind bars. It had been a
tense and quiet summer in Raccoon City, at least on
the surface. . . .

She glided past silent houses, the faint glow of
television sets spilling out across well-kept lawns, the
distant drone of crickets and an occasional barking
dog the only sounds in the air that whipped past her.
The uneasy citizens of Raccoon dwelled behind those
locked doors, waiting for the announcement that the

killers had been apprehended and that their city was safe.

If they only knew. . . .

For just a moment, Rebecca envied them their ignorance. She'd come to the rather disheartening conclusion in the last couple of weeks that knowing the truth wasn't all it was cracked up to be—particularly when no one believed it.

It had been a long, merciless thirteen days since the nightmare at the Spencer estate. The surviving S.T.A.R.S. had escaped treachery and death just to run up against a massive brick wall of scornful disbelief when they'd tried to tell their tale. Jill, Chris, Barry, and herself had been labeled drug addicts and worse in the local papers, undoubtedly at Umbrella's urging—and after their suspension, even the RPD had refused to believe them. Now, with Umbrella taking over the investigation of the fire, undoubtedly getting rid of the last of the evidence . . . it was as if everywhere the S.T.A.R.S. turned, Umbrella had been there first, greasing palms and covering tracks, making it impossible to get anyone to listen to their story.

Not that it would have been that simple anyway. One of the biggest, most respectable med research and pharmaceutical companies in the world—not to mention the primary source of income in Raccoon—conducting bio-weapons research in a secret lab, creating experimental monsters—if I didn't know better, I'd probably think I was crazy, too.

At least the absolute worst was over. With the lab destroyed, the attacks on Raccoon had stopped—and though the people responsible hadn't been held accountable yet, she figured it was only a matter of time. Umbrella was experimenting with dangerous stuff, and wouldn't be able to hide it from a S.T.A.R.S. investigation. She and the others just had to watch their backs until the home office sent backup.

Speaking of—ouch . . .

The pancake holster was poking into her ribcage. Rebecca adjusted it through the thin cotton of her shirt, hoping that after tonight she wouldn't have to carry the weapon anymore—a snub-nosed .38 revolver from Barry's collection. She couldn't speak for the others, but she hadn't had a decent night's sleep since they'd escaped the Spencer estate, and walking around armed all of the time wasn't her idea of safe.

Sighing inwardly, she took a left on Foster and pedaled through the shadows toward Barry's house, reminding herself that he'd probably called the meeting because he'd heard from the home office with orders. He would only say that there had been a "development" and to show up ASAP—and though she was trying not to let her imagination run away with her, she couldn't help the steady pulse of excitement that had knotted her stomach since he'd called.

Maybe they'll fly us to New York to brief the investigation team, or even to Europe for when they storm Umbrella's headquarters. . . .

Wherever they were sent, it had to be better than staying in Raccoon. The strain of looking over their shoulders had been getting to all of them. Chris seemed to think that Umbrella was waiting until the public eye was off the S.T.A.R.S. before making their move, though it was only a theory—and not exactly the most reassuring thought to fall asleep by. Chickenheart Vickers had skipped out of town after only two days, unable to take the pressure—and although Jill, Chris, and Barry had condemned Brad's cowardice, Rebecca was starting to wonder if maybe the Alpha pilot didn't have the right idea. It wasn't that she wanted Umbrella to walk, there was no question that their experiments were morally reprehensible and certainly illegal—but until the S.T.A.R.S. sent help, staying in Raccoon City was dangerous.

Not after tonight; just a little bit longer, and this will all be over. No more guns, no more locked doors—no more worrying about what Umbrella will do to us for knowing the truth.

When they'd first made the report, their superiors in New York had told them to stay put. Assistant Director Kurtz himself had promised to do some investigating and get back to them—but it had been eleven days, and still no word. She had no intention of running away as Brad had done, but she'd come to hate the feeling of that holster, the weight of the deadly steel against her side every waking moment of every day. She was supposed to be a *chemist*, for chrissake. . . .

And once the reinforcements come, maybe they'll move me to one of the labs, let me study the virus. Technically I'm still a Bravo; there's no way they'd want me on the front lines. . . .

There was no question that it would be the best use

of her talents. The others were experienced soldiers, but Rebecca had only been with the S.T.A.R.S. for five weeks. Her first mission had been the one to Raccoon Forest that had wiped out over half the team and clued the rest of them in to Umbrella's secret. Since then, she'd spent a lot of time brushing up on the molecular architecture of viruses, trying to determine the T-Virus replication strategy. The S.T.A.R.S. didn't need field medics right now, they needed scientists . . . and if she'd learned anything from the Spencer estate disaster, it was that she belonged in a lab. She'd held her own that night, but she also knew that working with the T-Virus was the greatest contribution she could make toward stopping Umbrella.

And you may as well face it, her mind whispered, *you're fascinated by it. The chance to study an unclassified emerging mutagen, to find out what makes it tick—that's what makes* you *tick.*

Yeah, well, there was no shame in enjoying her work. She'd joined the S.T.A.R.S. in hopes of just such an opportunity—and with any luck, after tonight's meeting she would be packing a bag and getting the hell out of Raccoon City, heading into a new phase of her life as a S.T.A.R.S. biochemist.

She pulled to a stop at the end of the block in front of a huge, two-story remodeled Victorian painted a pale yellow, checking all around for anything suspicious before getting off her bike. The Burtons lived next to a sprawling suburban park, heavy with trees. Even a few weeks ago, she might have wandered through the silent park, enjoying the balmy summer night, looking at the stars; now it was just one more dark place for someone to hide. Shivering slightly in spite of the warm, humid air, she hurried up the front walk.

Dragging her bike onto the porch, she wiped sweat from the back of her neck and checked her watch. She'd made excellent time, only twenty minutes since Barry's call. Rebecca leaned the bicycle against the railing, praying that he had good news.

Before she could knock, Barry opened the door, dressed in a T-shirt and jeans, his heavily muscled body filling the door's frame. Barry lifted weights. With a vengeance.

He smiled and stood back to let her inside, taking a quick look out at the quiet street before following her into the front hall. His Colt Python was tucked into a hip holster, making him look like an overgrown cowboy.

"You see anybody?" he asked lightly.

She shook her head. "No. I took back streets, too."

Barry nodded, and though he was still smiling a little, she could see the haunted look in his eyes, the look he'd had ever since their narrow escape. She wished she could tell him that nobody blamed him, but knew it wouldn't make a difference; Barry still held himself responsible for a lot of what had happened at the estate that night. He looked as though he was losing weight, too, though she figured that had more to do with him missing his wife and kids; he'd sent them out of town immediately following the incident, terrified for their safety.

Just one more way that Umbrella has damaged our lives. . . .

He led her through the spacious hallway past the stairs, the walls decorated with framed drawings in crayon that his daughters had made. The Burton house was rambling and spacious, filled with the scuffed and well-worn furnishings that epitomized family.

"Chris and Jill should be here any time. You want some coffee?"

He seemed tense, scruffing nervously at his short red beard.

"No, thanks. Maybe some water. . . ."

"Yeah, sure. Go ahead and introduce yourself, I'll be back in a minute." He hurried off to the kitchen before she could ask him if anything was wrong.

Introduce myself? What's going on?

She walked through the hall's arched opening into the cluttered, comfortable living room and stopped, a little startled to see a strange man sitting in one of the recliners. He stood up as she entered the room, smiling—but she could see by the way his dark gaze narrowed slightly that he was sizing her up.

Even a few weeks ago, the careful scrutiny would have made her horribly self-conscious. She was the youngest S.T.A.R.S. member ever to be accepted for active duty, and knew that she looked it—but if anything positive had come from the incident at the Umbrella lab, it was that she no longer cared much about things like social embarrassment. Facing down a house full of monsters tended to put things in perspective that way. Besides which, being stared at had gotten pretty routine since then.

She gazed back at him impassively, studying him in return. Jeans, a nice shirt, running shoes. He also wore a hip holster with a nine-millimeter Beretta, the S.T.A.R.S. standard-issue sidearm. He was tall, maybe a full foot over her five-foot three-inch frame, but slender, with a physique like a swimmer's. He was almost movie-star handsome, a high, weathered brow and finely chiseled features, short, dark hair and a piercing gaze that sparkled with intelligence.

"You must be Rebecca Chambers," he said. He had a British accent, his words clipped and somehow polished. "You're the biochemist, is that right?"

Rebecca nodded. "Working on it. And you are . . ."

He smiled wider, shaking his head. "Forgive my manners, please. I hadn't expected . . . that is, I . . ."

He stepped around Barry's low coffee table and extended his hand, flushing slightly. "I'm David Trapp, with the S.T.A.R.S. Exeter branch in Maine," he said.

Rebecca felt cool relief wash over her; the S.T.A.R.S. had sent help instead of calling, fine by her. She shook his hand, stifling a grin, knowing that her appearance had thrown him. Nobody expected an eighteen-year-old scientist, and while she'd gotten used to the surprised looks, she still took a kind of mischievous pleasure at catching people off guard.

"So, are you like the scout or something?" she asked.

Mr. Trapp frowned. "Sorry?"

"For the investigation—are there other teams already here, or did you come to check things out first, get the dirt on Umbrella . . ."

She trailed off as he shook his head slowly, almost sadly, his dark eyes glittering with an emotion she couldn't read.

It came out in his voice, heavy with frustrated anger—and as the words sank in, Rebecca felt her knees go watery with a sudden anxious dread.

"I'm sorry to have to tell you this, Ms. Chambers. I have reason to believe that Umbrella has gotten to key members of the S.T.A.R.S., either by bribery or blackmail. There is no investigation—and no one else is coming."

A look of confused terror passed through the girl's light brown eyes and just as quickly was gone. She took a deep breath and blew it out.

"Are you sure? I mean, did Umbrella try to get to you, or . . . are you *positive?*"

David shook his head. "I'm not absolutely certain, no—but I wouldn't be here if I wasn't . . . concerned about it."

It was a bit of an understatement, but David still wasn't past the shock of seeing how young she was, and felt an almost instinctive desire not to alarm her any further. Barry had mentioned that she was something of a child genius, but he hadn't really expected a *child*. The biochemist wore high tops and cut-off denim shorts rolled at the knee, topped by a shapeless black T-shirt.

Get past it; this child may be the only scientist we have left.

The thought rekindled the anger that had been burning in David's gut for the past few days. The story that had been unfolding since Barry's call wasn't a pretty one, filled with treachery and lies—and the fact that the S.T.A.R.S., *his* S.T.A.R.S., were involved . . .

Barry walked into the room with a glass of water and Rebecca took it from him gratefully, swallowing half of it in one gulp.

Barry shot him a glance and then turned his attention to Rebecca. "He told you, huh?"

The girl nodded. "Do Jill and Chris know?"

"Not yet. That's why I called," Barry said. "Look, no point in going through this twice. We should wait for them to show up before we get into specifics."

"Agreed," David said. He generally found that first impressions were the most telling, and if they were going to be working together, he wanted to get a feel for the girl's character.

The three of them sat, and Barry started to tell Rebecca how he and David had met back in S.T.A.R.S. training when they were both much younger men. Barry told a good story, even if it was only to kill time. David listened with half an ear as Barry related an anecdote about their graduation night, involving a rather humorless drill sergeant and several rubber snakes. The girl was relaxing, even enjoying the story of their childish prank—

*—seventeen years ago. She would have been cele-
brating her first birthday.*

Still, she had put her questions on hold at Barry's
request, even though David knew she had to be
anxious about what he'd told her. The ability to
retrain one's focus so quickly was an admirable trait,
one that he'd never fully mastered.

He'd been able to think of little else since his own
call to the S.T.A.R.S. AD. David's devotion to the
organization had made the apparent betrayal all the
more bitter, like a bad taste in his mouth that
wouldn't go away. The S.T.A.R.S. had been David's
life for almost twenty years, had given him all the
things he'd lacked growing up—a sense of self-worth,
a sense of purpose and integrity. . . .

*And just like that, the lives of dedicated men and
women,* my *life and life's work simply tossed aside as if
it meant nothing. How much did that cost? How much
did Umbrella have to pay to buy the S.T.A.R.S.'s
honor?*

David shook the anger, focusing his attention on
Rebecca. If all he'd learned was true, time was short
and their resources were now severely limited. His
motivations weren't as important right now as hers.

He could tell by the way she held herself that she
wasn't the shy or submissive type, and she was
obviously bright; her eyes fairly sparkled with it.
From what Barry had told him, she'd acted profes-
sionally throughout the Spencer facility operation.
Her file suggested that she was more than qualified to

work with a chemical virus, assuming that she was as good as the reports said—

—and assuming she has any desire to put her life in further danger.

That was going to be the sticking point. She hadn't been with the S.T.A.R.S. for very long, and knowing that they'd sold their people out probably wasn't going to overwhelm her with feelings of confidence for the job ahead. It would be just as easy for her to step out of the game now. For that matter, it would be the intelligent choice for all of them—

There was a knock at the door, presumably the other two Alphas. David's hand drifted down to the butt of his nine-millimeter as Barry went to answer. When he walked back in leading the S.T.A.R.S. team members, David relaxed, then stood up to be formally introduced.

"Jill Valentine, Chris Redfield—this is Captain David Trapp, military strategist for the Maine S.T.A.R.S. Exeter branch."

Chris was the marksman, if David remembered correctly, and Jill something of a covert B&E specialist. Barry said that the pilot, Brad Vickers, had skipped town shortly after the Spencer incident. No great loss, from what he could gather; the man sounded distinctly unreliable.

He shook hands with both of them and they all sat down, Barry nodding toward him.

"David's an old comrade of mine. We worked together on the same team for about two years, right after boot camp. He showed up on my doorstep about an hour ago with news, and I didn't think it could wait. David?"

David cleared his throat, trying to focus on the significant facts. After a pause, he began at the beginning.

"As you already know, six days ago, Barry placed several calls to various S.T.A.R.S. branches to see if any word had come from the home office about the tragedy that occurred here. I received one of those calls. It was the first I'd heard about it, and I've since found out that the New York office hasn't contacted anyone about your discovery. No warnings or memos. Nothing has been issued to the S.T.A.R.S. regarding the Umbrella Corporation."

Chris and Jill exchanged looks of concern.

"Maybe they're not done investigating," Chris said slowly.

David shook his head. "I spoke to the assistant director myself the day after Barry called. I didn't tell him about the contact, only that I'd heard rumor of a problem in Raccoon, and wanted to know if it had any merit. . . ."

He looked at the assembled group and sighed inwardly, feeling like he'd already gone over it a thousand times.

Only in my mind, searching for another answer . . . and there isn't one.

"The AD wouldn't tell me anything outright," he continued, "and he told me that I should remain quiet about it until official word came down. What he *would* say was that there had been a helicopter crash in

Raccoon City—and what he implied was that the surviving S.T.A.R.S. were trying to lay blame on Umbrella, angry over some sort of funding dispute."

"But that's not true!" Jill said. "We were investigating the murders, and found—"

"Yes, Barry told me," David interrupted. "You found that the murders were the result of a laboratory accident. The T-Virus that Umbrella was experimenting with was released somehow and it transformed the researchers into mad killers."

"That's exactly what happened," Chris said. "I know it sounds nuts, but we were there, we *saw* them."

David nodded. "I believe you. I have to admit, I was skeptical after speaking with Barry. As you say, it sounds 'nuts'—but my call to New York and what's happened since has changed all that. I've known Barry for a long time, and I knew that he wouldn't be looking to place blame for such an unfortunate incident unless Umbrella was, in fact, responsible. He even told me about his own unwilling involvement in the attempted cover up."

"But if Tom Kurtz told you that there was no conspiracy . . ." Chris said.

David sighed. "Yes. We have to assume that either our own organization has been misled—or that, like your Captain Wesker, members of the S.T.A.R.S. are now working for Umbrella."

There was a moment of shocked silence as they absorbed the information, and David could see anger and confusion play across their faces. He knew how they felt. It meant that the S.T.A.R.S. directors had either been manipulated by Umbrella or corrupted by them—and either way, the survivors of the Raccoon team had been hung out to dry, left vulnerable to whatever Umbrella might do.

God, if only I could believe that it was all a mistake. . . .

"Three days ago, I picked up a tail on my way in to work," he said softly. "I wasn't able to make them, but I'm assuming that they're some of Umbrella's people and that my call to New York was responsible."

"Have you tried to get hold of Palmieri?" Jill asked.

David nodded. The S.T.A.R.S. national commander was the one man he knew was above taking bribes; Marco Palmieri had been with the S.T.A.R.S. since the very beginning. "I was informed by his secretary that he's leading a classified operation in the Middle East and won't be available for months—and word has it that arrangements are being made for his retirement while he's away."

"You think Umbrella's behind it?" Chris asked.

David shrugged. "Umbrella *has* made substantial donations to the S.T.A.R.S. over the years, which means they have the contacts. If they're trying to turn the S.T.A.R.S. away from investigating them, getting rid of Dr. Palmieri would be to their advantage."

David glanced around the room, trying to assess their readiness for the rest of it. Barry's fists were clenched, and he stared at them as if he'd never seen them before. Jill and Rebecca both seemed lost in thought, though he could see that they had accepted his story as truth. It would save them time, at least. . . .

Chris stood up and started to pace, his youthful features flushed with anger. "So basically, we've got no credibility with the locals, no backup coming, and we've been branded as liars by our own people. The Umbrella investigation is dead and we're *screwed*, does that pretty much sum it up?"

David could see that the anger wasn't directed at him, just as the anger that *he* felt wasn't for the young Alpha. The thought of what Umbrella had done, what the S.T.A.R.S. were involved in—it made him sick with rage, with feelings of helplessness that he hadn't felt since his childhood.

Stop thinking of yourself. Tell them the rest.

David stood up and looked at Chris, though he addressed all of them. He hadn't even had time to tell Barry yet.

"Actually, there's more. It seems that there's another Umbrella facility on the Maine coast, conducting experiments with this virus of theirs—and just like what happened here, they've lost control."

David turned to Rebecca, taking in her wide, horrified gaze as he finished. "I'm taking a team in, without S.T.A.R.S. authorization—and I want you to come with us."

†wo

THEY ALL STARED AT DAVID, CHRIS FEELING
like he'd just been punched in the gut. He was still
reeling from the information about the S.T.A.R.S.,
from the realization that they were on their own—
and now another lab?

And he wants to take Rebecca. . . .

David went on, his dark gaze still fixed on the
young Bravo. "I've talked to the people on my team I
believe to be trustworthy, and three of them have
agreed to go. I'm not going to lie to you—it will be
dangerous, and without the S.T.A.R.S. to back us up,
there's no guarantee we'll be able to close the lab
down. We just want to go in, collect some solid
evidence on this T-Virus, and get back out before
anyone even knows we're—"

Before he could stop himself, Chris interrupted. "I'm going, too."

"We all go," Barry said firmly. Jill nodded, putting her arm around Rebecca. The teen seemed flustered, her cheeks red, and looking at her, Chris was once again reminded of Claire. It was more than just a physical resemblance; Rebecca had the same wit, the same spirited blend of courage and thoughtfulness that Chris's younger sister had. And since the Spencer estate disaster, Chris had come to feel just as protective of Rebecca. Too many of his friends had died already. Joseph, Richard, Kenneth, Forest, and Enrico—not to mention Billy Rabbitson; his body had never been found, but Chris had no doubts that Umbrella had killed him to keep him from talking. It wasn't that Rebecca couldn't handle herself . . .

. . . *but damn it, she's part of our team. No way she goes without us.*

David shook his head. "Look, this isn't a full-scale op; five people is already stretching it. Rebecca's got the background we need to find the data on the virus, and she already knows what symptoms to look for."

"You've got your team right here," Chris said. "You can take us instead, let your guys look into the cover up. . . ."

David sat back down and looked at Chris, his face expressionless. "Tell me who's involved in Umbrella's conspiracy to hide their research," he said.

Chris glanced at the others, then back at David, determined not to let his confusion show. "We suspect several people locally. Umbrella's office workers, of course. The police commissioner, Chief Irons, a couple of his men . . ."

David nodded. "And now that it looks like the S.T.A.R.S. are in on this, what do you propose to do?"

Where the hell is he going with this?

Chris sighed. "I don't know. I . . . we should contact the Feds, maybe an internal affairs division to look into the S.T.A.R.S. and the RPD—"

Barry cut in. "—and we'll get in touch with some of the other S.T.A.R.S. branches. There are still good people working out there who ain't gonna be too happy that Umbrella's taking over."

David nodded again. "So you agree that Umbrella has to be stopped, even though it will be dangerous?"

"Well, no shit," Chris said, scowling angrily. "We can't just sit around and do *nothing,* there's no telling what could happen if the T-Virus gets out again!"

"And what can *you* tell me about the classification of the virus?" David asked quietly.

Chris opened his mouth to answer—and then closed it, staring at David thoughtfully.

I was about to say, "You should ask Rebecca." And he knows it.

David stood up and looked at all of them in turn as he spoke, his voice intense and determined. "I agree, Umbrella has to be stopped—but let's not kid ourselves. We're talking about breaking from the S.T.A.R.S. and going up against a multi-billion dollar establishment on our own. *Nowhere* is going to be safe, and our only chance for success is if we each do what we can, what we're *good* at, to take Umbrella down."

He fixed his cool gaze on Chris, as if he realized that Chris was the one who had to be convinced. "You and Jill and Barry already know what to look for here, and you've been with the S.T.A.R.S. longer than Rebecca. You should stay here, out of sight, see if you can ferret out the connection between the local police and Umbrella—and reach out to the S.T.A.R.S. members that you think would help us."

David turned to Rebecca again. "And if you agree, I think we should leave for Maine tonight. With the information I have, it looks as though things have already gotten out of hand. My team is standing by; we could go in tomorrow at dusk."

The room was silent for a moment, the only sound that of the ceiling fan whirring overhead. Chris still felt angry, but couldn't find a hole in the man's logic; he was right about their options, and whether Chris liked it or not, the choice to go to Maine was Rebecca's to make.

"What information *do* you have?" Jill asked thoughtfully. "How did you find out about the lab?"

David reached down to a battered briefcase propped next to his chair and dug through it, pulling out a file folder. "An interesting story in itself, if a strange one. I was hoping that one of you might be able to decipher some of this. . . ."

He laid out three sheets of paper on the coffee table as he spoke, what looked like photocopies of newspaper clippings, and a simple diagram. "Shortly after I talked to the home office, I received a visit from a stranger, a man who claimed to be a friend of the S.T.A.R.S. . . . he told me his name was Trent, and gave me these."

"Trent!" Jill broke in excitedly. She turned to Chris, her eyes wide, and Chris felt his heart skip a beat. He'd almost forgotten about their mysterious benefactor.

The guy who told Jill to watch out for traitors, who told Brad where to pick us up. . . .

David stared at Jill, his expression puzzled. "You know him?"

"Just before we went in to rescue the Bravos, a man named Trent gave me some information about the Spencer estate, and warned me about Wesker," Jill said. "He was quite a piece of work, real shady—he didn't give anything away, you know? But he knew what was going on with Umbrella, and what he *did* tell me all panned out."

Barry nodded. "And Brad Vickers said that Trent called in the estate's coordinates right after Wesker activated the triggering system. If he hadn't radioed, we woulda blown up with the rest of the mansion."

Chris suddenly realized that he had a serious headache brewing as they all gathered around Barry's coffee table, staring down at the papers. The S.T.A.R.S. were working for Umbrella, there was another T-Virus facility operating in Maine—and now Trent again, popping up like some cryptic fairy godmother, his motives impossible to guess at. It was like some kind of a game, the stakes all or nothing as they struggled to get to the bottom of Umbrella's conspiracy.

And we have no choice but to play—but whose game are we playing? And what do we risk losing if we fail?

Chris shot an unhappy glance at Rebecca, thinking again of his kid sister and wishing, not for the first time, that they'd never heard of Umbrella.

David watched them study the information that Trent had given him, somehow not surprised that the enigmatic stranger had contacted the S.T.A.R.S. before. The man had been a professional, though at *what,* precisely, David couldn't imagine.

Why would he want to help us fight Umbrella? What's in it for him?

David thought back to the brief encounter he'd had only five days ago, searching his memory for some additional clues, something he'd missed. He'd arrived home late from work, and it had been raining . . .

. . . *pouring, a thundering summer storm that beat at the windows and masked the sound of his gentle knocking.* . . .

The Exeter S.T.A.R.S. had enjoyed an easy summer, more paperwork than action. The Bravos had taken off for a criminal profiling seminar in New Hampshire, and David had been entertaining thoughts of packing a bag and attending the final days—until he'd received Barry's call, followed by his first hint from the home office that something was wrong.

He'd spent the next day calling a few of his branch contacts with discreet questions and digging through files on Umbrella, not making it home until almost midnight. The driving rain had ushered him into his cold, dark house, the atmosphere matching his mood perfectly. He'd poured a scotch and collapsed on the couch, his head spinning from the implications of what he'd learned—that either his old friend Barry was lying or that the AD for the S.T.A.R.S. was. . . .

The rapping at his door was so soft that he missed it at first, the steady rain hammering on the roof covering the sound. Then it grew louder.

Frowning, David looked at his watch and walked slowly to the door, wondering who the hell came calling in the middle of the night. He lived alone and had no family; it had to be work, or maybe someone with car trouble. . . .

He cracked the door open—and saw a man in a black trench coat standing on his porch, streams of water running down his lined face.

The stranger smiled, an open, friendly expression, his eyes glittering bright with humor. "David Trapp?"

David took in the man at a glance. Tall and thin, maybe a few years past David's age, say forty-two or forty-three. His dark hair was plastered to his skull by the rain, and he held a large manila envelope in one gloved hand.

"Yes?"

The man grinned wider. "My name is Trent, and this is for you."

He held out the damp envelope and David glanced at it warily, not sure if he should take it. Mr. Trent didn't seem dangerous, or at least not threatening . . . but he was still a stranger, and David preferred to know the people he accepted gifts from.

"Do I know you?" David asked.

Trent shook his head, his smile unwavering. "No. But I know *you,* Mr. Trapp. And I also know what you're about to go up against. Believe me, you're going to need all the help you can get."

"I don't know what you're talking about. Perhaps you have me confused with someone else—"

Trent's smile faded as he extended the envelope, his dark eyes narrowing slightly. "Mr. Trapp, it's raining. And this is for you."

Confused and not a little irritated, David opened the door wider to accept the envelope. As soon as he grasped it, Trent turned and started to walk away.

"Hold on a moment—"

Trent ignored him, disappearing into the rain-drenched shadows around the side of the house.

David stood in the doorway uncertainly, holding the damp paper and staring into the pouring darkness for another minute before going back inside. Once he'd studied the contents, he wished he'd gone after Trent—but by then, of course, it was too late.

Too late and only too obvious what he'd meant. He knew about Umbrella and the S.T.A.R.S.—but who does he work for? And why did he choose to contact me?

Jill and Rebecca were studying the map while Barry and Chris worked through the copied newspaper articles. There were four of them, all recent, all centered around the tiny coastal town of Caliban Cove, Maine. Three of them concerned the disappearances of local fishermen, all presumed dead. The fourth was a rather humorous piece about the "ghosts" that haunted the cove; it seemed that several townspeople had heard strange sounds floating across the waters late at night, described as "the cries of the damned." The writer of the article had laughingly suggested that the witnesses to the phenomena should probably stop drinking their mouthwash before bed.

Funny. Unless you know what we know about Umbrella.

The map was of the stretch of coast just south of the small town, an aerial sketch of the cove itself. David had uncovered a few facts about the area on a visit to Exeter's library, uncomfortable using the S.T.A.R.S. computer after Barry's call. The rather isolated stretch had been privately owned for several years, bought up by an anonymous group. There was a defunct lighthouse on the northern rim of the inlet, sitting atop a cliff that was supposedly riddled with sea caves.

Trent's map showed several structures behind and below the lighthouse, leading down to a small pier on the southern tip of the open crescent. There was a notched border that ran the length of the cove on the inland side, presumably a fence. CALIBAN COVE was written across the top in bold letters. In smaller type just beneath were the words UMB. RESEARCH AND TESTING.

The third piece of paper that Trent had given him was the one that David didn't understand; there was a short list of names at the top, seven in all:

LYLE AMMON, ALAN KINNESON, TOM ATHENS, LOUIS THURMAN, NICOLAS GRIFFITH, WILLIAM BIRKIN, TIFFANY CHIN.

Just under it was a somewhat poetic list of sorts, set into the center of the page in curling font.

Jill had picked it up again and was reading it carefully. She looked up at David, a half-smile on her face.

"No question that we've got the same Trent here. The guy's into riddles."

"Any idea what it means?" David asked.

Jill sighed heavily. "Well, one of the names here was in the material that Trent gave me—William Birkin. We figured out that at least some of the others were researchers at the Spencer facility, so I'm willing to bet these people also work for Umbrella. Birkin may not have been at the estate when it was destroyed. I don't recognize any of the others. . . ."

David nodded. "I checked all of them with the S.T.A.R.S. database and came up blank. The rest, though . . . *Is* it a riddle of some sort?"

Jill glanced back at the paper, frowning as she read it to herself again:

Ammon's message received/blue series/enter answer for key/letters and numbers reverse/time rainbow/don't count/blue to access.

Rebecca took the paper from her as Jill looked back at David thoughtfully. "A lot of what Trent gave me seemed like pretty random stuff, but some of it related to the Spencer mansion's secrets; the whole place was rigged with puzzle locks and traps. Maybe this is the same deal. It relates to something you'll find—"

"Oh, shit."

They all turned to Rebecca who was staring at the top of the page, her face drained of color. She looked at David with an expression of anxious despair.

"Nicolas Griffith is on this list."

David nodded. "You know who he is?"

She looked around at all of them, her young face openly distressed. "Yeah, except I thought he was dead. He was one of the greats, one of the most brilliant men ever to work in the biosciences."

She turned back to David, her gaze heavy with dread. "If he's with Umbrella, we've got a lot more to worry about than the T-Virus getting out. He's a genius in the field of molecular virology—and if the stories are true, he's also totally insane."

Rebecca looked back at the list, her stomach a leaden knot.

Dr. Griffith, still alive . . . and involved with Umbrella. Could today possibly get any worse?

"What can you tell us about him?" David asked.

Rebecca's mouth felt dry. She reached for her glass of water and drained it before looking at David.

"How much do you know about the study of viruses?" she asked.

He smiled a little. "Nothing. That's why I'm here."

Rebecca nodded, trying to think of where to start. "Okay. Viruses are classified by their replication strategy and by the type of nucleic acid in the virion—that's the specialized element in a virus that allows it to transfer its genome to another living cell. A genome is a single, simple set of chromosomes. According to the Baltimore Classification, there are seven distinct types of viruses, and each group infects certain organisms in a certain way.

"In the early sixties, a young scientist at a private university in California challenged the theory, insisting that there was an eighth group—one based loosely on dsDNA *and* ssDNA viruses—that could infect *everything* it contacted. It was Dr. Griffith. He published several papers, and while it turned out that he was wrong, his reasoning was brilliant. I know, I read them. The scientific community scoffed at his theory, but his research on virus-specified inclusion bodies in the cytoplasm without a linear genome . . ."

Rebecca trailed off, noticing the blank expressions on their faces. "Sorry. Anyway, Griffith stopped trying to prove the theory, but a lot of people were interested to see what he'd come up with next."

Jill interrupted, frowning. "Where did you learn all this?"

"In school. One of my professors was kind of a science-history buff. His specialty was defunct theories . . . and scandals."

"So what happened?" David asked.

"The next time anyone heard from Griffith, it was because he'd gotten kicked out of the university. Dr. Vachss—that was my prof—told us that Griffith was *officially* fired for using drugs, methamphetamines— but the rumor was that he'd been experimenting with drug-induced behavior modification on a couple of his students. Neither of them would talk, but one of them ended up in an asylum and the other eventually committed suicide. Nothing was ever proved, but after that, no one would hire him—and as far as the facts go, that's the last anyone heard of Nicolas Griffith."

"But there's more to the story?" David asked.

Rebecca nodded slowly. "In the mid-eighties, a private lab in Washington was broken into by cops and the bodies of three men were found, all dead of a filovirus infection—it was Marburg, one of the most lethal viruses there is. They'd been dead for weeks; neighbors had complained because of the smell. The papers the police found in the lab suggested that all three men were research assistants to a Dr. Nicolas Dunne, and that they had allowed themselves to be deliberately infected with what *they* understood to be a harmless cold virus. Dr. Dunne was going to see if he could cure it."

She stood up, crossing her arms tightly. The agony those men must have endured; she'd seen pictures of Marburg victims.

From the initial headache to extreme amplification in a matter of days. Fever, clotting, shock, brain damage, massive hemorrhaging from every orifice—they would've died in pools of their own blood. . . .

"And your professor thought it was Griffith?" Jill asked softly.

Rebecca forced the images away and turned to Jill, finishing the story the way Dr. Vachss had. "Griffith's mother—her maiden name was Dunne."

Barry let out a low whistle, as Jill and Chris exchanged a worried look. David was studying her intently, his gaze cool and unreadable. All the same, she thought she knew what was going through his mind.

He's wondering if this changes things. If I'll go with him to see this Caliban Cove facility, now that I know it's being run by people like Griffith.

Rebecca looked away from David's intense scrutiny and saw that the rest of her team was watching her, their faces tight with concern. Since that terrible night at the Spencer estate, they'd become like a family to her. She didn't want to leave, to risk never seeing them again. . . .

. . . but David's right. Without the support of the S.T.A.R.S., nowhere will be safe for any of us. And this would be my chance to contribute, to do what I'm good at. . . .

She wanted to believe that it was the only reason,

that she'd be going to fight the good fight—but she couldn't help the tiny shiver of excitement that ran through her at the thought of getting her hands on the T-Virus. It would be a golden opportunity to study the mutagen before anyone else, to categorize the effects and pick apart the virion right down to its smallest capsid.

Rebecca took a deep breath and blew it out, her decision made.

"I'll do it," she said. "When do we go?"

THREE

JILL FELT HER HEART QUICKEN AT REBEC-
ca's words, a feeling that things were happening too
fast and that they weren't prepared. Her decision
seemed sudden, even though Jill really hadn't
doubted that she'd volunteer; Rebecca was a lot
stronger than she looked.

She glanced around Barry's wide, open living room,
discreetly noting the reactions of her teammates.
Chris's face was strained, his mouth drawn as he
stared absently at the map of Caliban Cove, while
Barry walked across to one of the living room windows, staring out past the curtain and scowling at
nothing in particular.

*They're worried about her, and maybe they should
be; Griffith sounds like a serious psycho . . . but would
any of us have hesitated if we'd been asked to go?*

It just proved that Rebecca was as committed as they were, also no great surprise. Getting to know the young Bravo had been one of the only bright spots in the frustrating days since the mansion had burned. The girl had been unfailingly optimistic about their chances against Umbrella even after their suspension, and had worked tirelessly to keep all of their spirits up. She was brilliant, too—and yet she never flaunted it, or came across as condescending when she was attempting to discuss aspects of the T-Virus with them.

Rebecca looked a bit distraught herself, glancing around at the three men in the room. Even David Trapp seemed vaguely uncomfortable with her decision, probably because of Rebecca's youth. . . .

Men. She's young, she's cute, and she's undoubtedly smarter than all of us put together—but the young and cute part tends to make them overlook the rest.

Jill caught her eye and smiled encouragingly. At Rebecca's age, Jill had been a professional thief, and a good one. She was worried about Rebecca, too, but only because she'd grown to care about her. The fact that she was a young woman wasn't a reason to underestimate her talents.

Rebecca smiled back, and walked over to sit by her as David nodded hesitantly at his newest teammate.

"All right, then. Good. There's a plane leaving for Bangor at twenty-three hundred hours, with a connecting flight to a field just outside of Exeter. I thought we could all go over a bit of strategy here, and then drop by your place on the way to the airfield so you can pack a few things."

Rebecca nodded, and after cracking a window open, Barry moved back to join them, leaning against one arm of the couch. He folded his arms across his massive chest and jerked his chin toward David.

"You're the strategist," he said, not unkindly. "Why don't you start us off?"

The respect between the two men was obvious, making Jill like David all the more. In spite of Barry's screw ups in the Spencer fiasco, Jill had grown to trust him, something she didn't do easily—and he seemed confident in David Trapp's skills.

"I don't mean to take over," David said, "but I have a few thoughts on how we might approach this situation. I've known about the S.T.A.R.S.'s betrayal for several days now . . . though I thought we all might spend a few moments considering our course of action. I realize that this must come as quite a shock."

Jill picked up on the same thread of bitterness she'd noticed earlier, on the word "betrayal." The fact that the S.T.A.R.S. were in bed with Umbrella obviously wasn't sitting too well with Mr. Trapp . . .

. . . probably not with Chris or Barry, either. Both of them have more time invested with the S.T.A.R.S. than me or Becca. . . .

Jill was disappointed and angry that the S.T.A.R.S. had sold out, but it wasn't going to be a factor in her decision to work at bringing Umbrella down. Her path had been determined on the day that the McGee sisters had been brutally murdered. The two little girls were the first innocent victims of the T-Virus spill at the Spencer estate—and they had been her friends.

She pushed the thoughts away, focusing on the matter at hand. Without the S.T.A.R.S., their job *was* going to be a lot tougher. Not impossible, but she had to admit to herself that their chance of success had just dropped to somewhere near zero. It was a good thing she didn't mind being the underdog.

It doesn't matter anyway. Umbrella's going to pay for what they've done, one way or another. . . .

Barry's gruff voice broke the quiet in the room, his gaze thoughtful. "Maybe we should go to the press. Not local, but someone big, national—"

David sighed, shaking his head. "I thought of that. It's a good idea, but right now we don't have the proof to make anything stick."

"Yeah, but at least Umbrella wouldn't move on us with everyone watching."

"We couldn't count on that," Jill said. "If they got to the S.T.A.R.S., they could get to anyone. And without evidence . . . well, you gotta admit, the story's the kind of thing even the tabloids wouldn't buy."

There was a moment of sullen silence, as if her words reminded them all of how insane it sounded— how insane it would sound to anyone who hadn't experienced what they'd been through.

A virus that accidentally turns people into zombies,

being used to create unspeakable monsters as living weapons . . . invented and then covered up by a major corporation that hires mad scientists to experiment on human beings. All it needs is a Nazi war criminal with an atomic weapon, we'd have a best-seller on our hands. . . .

"Well, what we were talking about before—organizing some of the other S.T.A.R.S.," Chris said. "I've got a few people in mind, some of the guys I trained with. And I know Barry's got a lot of contacts."

David nodded agreement. "Yes, I think that should be a priority. My concern is how to get in touch with them. The branch offices may already be tapped, and we want to keep Umbrella from learning about our plans for as long as possible. Unfortunately, we won't have use of the S.T.A.R.S.'s resources for much longer."

"Maybe we should look for a go-between," Jill said slowly. "Someone who doesn't have ties to the S.T.A.R.S. . . ."

Chris grinned suddenly. "I know a guy from back in the Air Force who works for Jack Hamilton now, one of the section heads for the FBI—I don't know much about Hamilton, but Pete's about as honest as they come. And he owes me a favor."

"Brilliant," David said. "Perhaps you could ask him to help you look into the local police as well. Once we have solid evidence from the Maine facility, we can go to your friend, instigate a federal investigation."

It sounded good, but Jill found herself feeling frustrated by the talk. She wanted to act. Waiting for the S.T.A.R.S. to contact them had been bad enough; knowing that Rebecca was going to be risking her life while they waited idly by would be excruciating.

"You said you had some thoughts about what else we could do," she said.

David nodded. "Yes, though once we involve the government, it may not come to anything quite so daring. I had been formulating a plan to infiltrate Umbrella headquarters, a risky proposition at best. It seems wisest to work on a smaller scale for now—but I *do* believe the three of you should drop out of sight, as soon as possible. I also think it would be prudent for you to see what you can uncover on Mr. Trent— though I have the distinct feeling that you won't come up with much, if anything. . . ."

He smiled a little, and having met Trent, Jill understood his doubts perfectly. Their strange bene- factor had struck her as a very careful man.

"I get the impression that we'll only find what he wants us to find," David continued, "but it is worth a look. And we'll need to arrange for a rendezvous site after we've—"

His soft, musical voice broke off suddenly as he tilted his head to one side, listening intently. Jill heard it in the same instant and felt her heart freeze in her chest.

A rustling in the bushes outside the window that Barry had opened.

Umbrella.

"Get down!" Jill shouted, and rolled off the couch, pulling Rebecca with her as the window shattered, the curtains blown aside in an explosive burst from an automatic rifle.

David dove for the floor as bullets riddled the chair he'd been in, already grabbing for his weapon. Tufts of padding floated past his wide eyes as a smoking trail of holes tore across the wall, plaster and wood flying.

Bloody hell—

There was a split-second break in the onslaught, just long enough for them to hear the crash of glass breaking from the back of the house.

"Barry, lights!" he shouted, but Barry was way ahead of him, the thunder of his Colt revolver drowning out the intermittent spray of the machine gun.

Boom! Boom!

The room went dark as Barry's rounds found their mark, glass raining down from above. Light still streamed into the darkness from the hall, and there was another hail of bullets from outside.

Chris scrabbled on elbows and knees for the hallway and in one smooth movement rolled onto his side and took out the additional lights. The living room was now completely black, and the bursts of automatic fire stopped.

Over the ringing in his ears, David heard boots crunching on glass from back in the kitchen. The heavy steps paused, the intruder probably waiting for the window shooter to catch up—

—and there will be more than two, covering the

exits. Kitchen door, front porch, someone watching the windows—

Another set of steps entered the kitchen, these hurried and shuffling, but they also stopped. The pair was waiting, either for more of their team or for the assembled S.T.A.R.S. to make a move. David's thoughts raced independently of him, reflexively considering and rejecting theories and options at lightning speed.

We get upstairs, pick them off one at a time—

—unless they mean to torch the house—

—so we run straight through them, out the back—

—except they've got the firepower advantage, maybe spook eyes and we'd be moving targets, no contest . . .

All he knew for certain was that they couldn't stay where they were. There was no cover for when the thugs got tired of waiting.

There was shuffling movement from the right as Barry's hulking shadow crouched toward him. David's eyes had adjusted enough to see Jill and Rebecca on the other side of the coffee table, both of them crouched and holding handguns. He couldn't make Chris out, but he was probably still by the hall.

Barry's house was the last on the block, a wooded park just past. If they could slip out, get into the trees—

The thought stuck; even a bad plan was better than none at all, and they didn't have time to work out alternatives.

"Basement door?" David whispered.

Barry's gruff voice was soft and strained. "Yeah."

No good, it would be posted. They'd have to get out through the second floor.

"We go through the park," he whispered quickly. "Jill, get to Chris and prepare to lay cover on my signal. Barry, Rebecca, as soon as we start, hit the stairs fast to an east window, softest jump. We'll follow. Ready? *Go.*"

Jill was already moving around the couch, disappearing silently into the thick shadows, Barry and Rebecca right behind. David paused just long enough to scoop up the papers that Trent had given him. He stuffed them inside his shirt, the crinkling pages cool against his sweaty skin. Nothing else in his briefcase would be damaging.

He crept toward the yawning blackness of the opening to the hall, edging to where Jill and Chris were crouched. The entry faced the side of the stairs. To the left was the front door and the foot of the steps. To the right, the quiet kitchen at the end of the long hall where the two Umbrella operatives waited.

They go right, I'll take left, when the shooting begins the rest of the strike force should rush the front door. . . .

David hoped. If the timing wasn't perfect, they were dead. Away from the faint light from the windows, it was too dark for hand signals. He leaned close between Jill and Chris, pitching his voice as low as possible.

"Both right, Jill low and outside," he whispered. They wouldn't be aiming for the floor, and Chris could use the wall of the entry as a shield. "I've got the front door. Keep it up for—six seconds *exactly*, no more. On zero, you need to be on the stairs, out of the corridor. On my mark . . . *now!"*

The three of them sprang into position, Chris and Jill firing toward the kitchen, David whirling to the left. He ran for the front door in a low crouch, the count ticking.

. . . *five . . . four . . .*

Behind him, Barry and Rebecca lunged for the stairs through the crash of bullets. David trained the Beretta on the darkness in front of him—and was only a foot away from the door when someone kicked it open.

Bam!

His shoulder connected with the heavy wood and he threw himself into it, slamming it closed. He dropped to the floor and jammed his heel against the base.

. . . *two . . .*

He fired into the door at an upward angle, five shots as fast as he could pull the trigger. There was a strangled scream, the sound of something heavy hitting the porch, and he fired three more before rolling to his feet, into the alcove at the foot of the stairs and out of the line of fire. Their time was up.

David spun, saw Jill and Chris already on their way up—and as his feet hit the first riser, there was a sound like an explosion behind him. The front door was suddenly a mass of flying splinters, heavy rounds tearing through the wood as the Umbrella team sought to end the battle. If the two Alphas hadn't killed the men in the kitchen, they were surely dead by now.

Halfway up the staircase, David turned and fired twice more through the rapidly disintegrating door, hoping he'd bought the S.T.A.R.S. enough time to escape.

Ten, maybe twenty seconds before they realize we're gone.

It was going to be close.

Rebecca stood on the dark landing, her heart pounding almost as loudly as the booming shots that chased Jill and Chris up the stairs.

Come on, come on—

Barry was to her right at the end of the landing's hall, barely visible by the moonlight that streamed through the open window. Jill was the first to reach the top. Rebecca steered her toward Barry with a touch, Chris following close behind.

Bam! Bam!

The muzzle on David's nine-millimeter flashed brightly in the darkness on the stairs, and then he was in front of her, materializing out of the gloom like a sweaty ghost.

"This way—"

Rebecca turned and ran for the window, David at her side. Jill had already gone and Chris was halfway out, Barry gripping one of his hands as he struggled to balance himself.

Please God, let there be a mattress, a pile of leaves— BOOM!

The crash of the front door flying open was followed by heavy footsteps and muffled male voices, angry and commanding. Chris disappeared through the window and then Barry was reaching for her, his mouth a grim line. She jammed her pistol back in its holster and stepped to the window.

Barry's warm hand on her back, Rebecca crawled onto the sill and looked down. There were hedges against the side of the house, lush and thick and impossibly far below. She caught a glimpse of Jill, standing on the lawn, aiming her weapon toward the front of the house and Chris looking up at them, his face tight with strain—

—*don't think just do it*—

Rebecca slid out the window, Barry's strong fingers finding her hand. Her shoulder groaned as gravity did its work, Barry leaning out to give her less of a drop, her body suspended in mid-air.

He let go and before she could feel real terror, she hit the bushes. There was small pain, twigs and branches scratching at her bare legs, and then Chris was pulling her out, lifting her easily from the twining hedges.

"Take the back," he breathed, his attention already fixed back on the window.

Rebecca snatched the revolver out as she stepped onto the lawn, turning to face the shadows that made up the backyard. To her left, a dark stand of trees stood maybe twenty meters away, silent and still.

Hurry, hurry. . . .

There was a thundering rattle of bullets inside the

house and a thrashing *thump* in the bushes to her right, but she didn't turn, intent on her assigned task.

A movement, by the corner of the house. Rebecca didn't hesitate, sending two shots into the thickening of shadow, Barry's .38 jerking in her hands. The figure crumpled, falling forward just enough for her to see that she'd hit a man clutching a rifle—and that he wasn't going to get up again.

—never shot anybody before—

"*Move!*" Chris shouted, and Rebecca jerked her head around, saw Barry climb out of the bushes and stumble toward them. There was a shout from the window, followed by a burst from an automatic rifle. Rebecca actually *felt* the bullets hit the ground near her feet, tearing up chunks of overgrown lawn. Dirt pelted her legs.

Shit!

David and Jill fired back as they ran for the trees, Chris leading the way. The shooter either ducked or was shot; the dull clatter of the rifle fell silent. As they reached the first of the wooded shadows, Rebecca heard the wail of approaching sirens—followed closely by shouts and running steps across Barry's front porch. Seconds later, there was a squeal of tires.

Rebecca stumbled through the brushy copse, dodging between narrow, gnarled trunks, trying to keep the others in sight. The revolver felt too heavy in her slick grasp and her entire body seemed to be pounding, her legs shaking, her breathing sharp and shallow. Everything had happened so fast. She'd known they were in danger, that Umbrella wanted them out of the way—

but knowing something wasn't the same as really *believing* it, as believing that violent strangers would break into Barry's home and try to take their lives. . . .

. . . and I may have taken one of theirs instead.

The thought that she might have killed someone . . . she forced it away before it could take hold, concentrating on the pale shape of Chris's T-shirt ahead. Her conscience would have to wait until she had time to think it through.

Ahead of them, the thick woods opened into a clearing, playground equipment gleaming dully in the pallid light. Chris slowed to a jog and then stopped where the line of trees ended, turning back to search the shadows for the rest of them.

Rebecca caught up to him, Barry and Jill just behind her, all of them breathing heavily and looking as stunned and sober as Rebecca felt.

"David, where's David?" Chris gasped, and as they all turned, straining to see past the dark, reaching branches, Rebecca saw one of the shadows to their left move. A stealthy, sliding movement.

"Look out!"

She dropped to the ground even as she yelled, fresh terror surging through her system—

—and the shadow fired at them, twice, the shots muted compared to the explosive thunder at the house. There was a third shot, louder, closer, and the shadow stumbled and fell, crashing against a tree before collapsing silently to the dirt. Except for the rising moan of sirens, the park was again still.

Rebecca slowly raised her head, craning to look over her shoulder and saw David, standing, still pointing his Beretta at the fallen shooter. Jill and Chris were crouched next to her, both of them holding their weapons out, staring around them with wide, searching gazes—

—and on her other side, Barry was sprawled on the ground, his face pressed to the blanket of dried pine needles and long dead leaves.

He wasn't moving.

FOUR

THERE WAS DARKNESS FOR AN INDETERMI-
nate time, silent and complete—and then there were
voices, drawing him up through the black depths of
his limbo, voices that his floating mind couldn't
identify at first. From somewhere far away, he heard
sirens.

he's been hit
oh my God
see if it's clear
wait I can't find the wound help me—Barry? Barry,
can

"Barry, can you hear me?"
Rebecca. Barry opened his eyes and then closed
them immediately, wincing as the throbbing pain
wrapped around his skull. There was another pain in
his left arm, sharp and insistent but not as complete

as the ache in his head. He'd had acquaintance with both kinds of pain before.

Got shot, met up with a tree . . . or some asshole with a baseball bat.

He tried opening his eyes again as small hands moved across his chest, lightly searching. It took him a second to focus on the worried faces looming over him, Jill and Chris and a frightened-looking Rebecca, her fingers probing his shirt for the wound. The sirens had fallen mercifully silent, though he could hear the cop cars pulling up his street, their powerfully revving engines echoing through the wooded park.

"Left bicep," he mumbled, and started to sit up. The dark woods wavered unsteadily, and then Rebecca was gently pushing him back down.

"Don't move," she said firmly. "Just lay there a second, okay? Chris, give me your shirt."

"But Umbrella—" Barry started.

"It's clear," David said, kneeling next to the others. "Be still."

Rebecca lifted his arm carefully, looking at both sides. Barry flexed his arm slightly and scowled at the burst of pain, but could tell it wasn't bad; the bone was still intact.

"Right out the deltoid," Rebecca said. "Looks like you're gonna have to lay off the weights for awhile."

Her tone was light, but he could see the concern in her gaze as she studied his face. She started wrapping Chris's T-shirt tightly around his arm, watching him intently.

"You've got a nasty bump on your temple," she said. "How do you feel?"

Though his head was still pounding, the pain had subsided to ache status. He felt light-headed and a little nauseous, but he still knew his own name and what day of the week it was; if it was a concussion, he wasn't impressed.

I've had worse hangovers. . . .

"Pretty much like shit," he said, "but I'm okay. I must've hit a tree on the way down."

As she finished the makeshift bandage, he sat up again, this time with better results. They had to get moving before the cops decided to search the woods—but where could they go? It seemed unlikely that Umbrella would attack twice in one night, but it wasn't a theory worth testing. None of their homes would be safe. At least his family was out of harm's way visiting Kathy's parents in Florida. The thought that they could have just as easily been at home, his girls playing in their rooms when the shooting had started—

He staggered unsteadily to his feet, finding strength in the rage that he'd lived with since that night at the estate. Wesker had threatened Kathy and the girls to force Barry's cooperation in Umbrella's coverup, using him to get to the underground laboratories. Barry's guilt had blossomed into fury in the days since, an anger that transcended any he'd ever known.

"Bastards," Barry snarled. "Goddamn Umbrella *bastards.*"

The others stood up with him, Chris's bare chest

pale in the faint light, all of them seeming relieved
that he wasn't badly hurt—except for David, who
looked as unhappy as Barry had ever seen him. His
shoulders sagged from some unknown burden and
when he spoke, he wouldn't meet Barry's gaze.

"The man who shot you," David said. He held up a
nine-millimeter with a suppressor attached, blood
spattered across the barrel. "I killed him. I—Barry,
it's Jay Shannon."

Barry stared at him. He heard the words, but was
unable to accept them. It wasn't possible.

"No. You didn't get a good look, it's too dark . . ."

David turned and walked through the trees, leading
them to the body of the shooter. Barry stumbled after
him, his head suddenly aching from more than just
smacking it on a tree trunk.

*It can't be Shannon, there's no way—David's rattled
from the attack, that's all, he made a mistake. . . .*

. . . except David didn't rattle under fire, he never
had, and he didn't make mistakes that easily. Barry
grit his teeth against the pain and followed, for once
hoping that his friend was wrong.

The man had collapsed on his back or David had
rolled him over. Either way, he stared up at them with
lifeless eyes, a random pine needle stuck to one of the
glazed orbs. The semi-jacketed round from David's
Beretta had punched a hole directly over his heart; it
had been a lucky shot. Looking down at the shooter's
ashen face, Barry felt his own heart turn to stone.

Jesus, Shannon, why? Why this?

"Who is he?" Jill asked softly.

Barry stared down at the dead man, unable to answer. David's reply seemed hollow, toneless.

"Captain Jay Shannon of the Oklahoma City S.T.A.R.S. Barry and I trained with him."

Barry found his voice, still looking at Jay's still face. "I called him last week, when I called David. He was worried about us, said he'd keep an eye out for Umbrella . . ."

. . . and we shot the shit for another couple of minutes, catching up, telling old stories. I told him I'd send pictures of the kids, and he said that he had to get off the phone, that he wanted to talk but he had a meeting. . . .

Umbrella must have already got to him, and the realization was cold and brutal and suddenly, horribly complete. Umbrella may have been behind the attack—but the S.T.A.R.S. had carried it out. Barry's home had been blown to hell by people they knew, and he'd been shot by a man he'd thought was a friend.

The solemn quiet was broken by the barking of dogs, faint through the shadowy trees. From the number and location, it sounded like the RPD K-9 unit had just reached his house. Barry looked away from the corpse, his thoughts returning to the immediate situation. They had to move.

"Where can we go?" David asked quickly. "Is there somewhere Umbrella wouldn't think to look, a cabin, an empty building . . . someplace we can get to on foot?"

Brad!

"Chickenheart's lease isn't up for a couple of months," Barry said. "His place is empty. And it's less than a mile from here."

David nodded briskly. "Let's go."

Barry turned toward the park's playground, leading the others across the moonlit clearing. There was a small trail that let out two blocks away, hopefully far enough away from the action that the cops wouldn't follow. Barry had walked through the park a million times, his wife at his side, his children dancing at their feet. . . .

. . . my home. This is my home, and it won't ever be the same again.

As they ran through the warm, peaceful night, Barry felt the hole in his arm start to bleed again. He clapped his right hand over the sticky dressing without slowing, letting the pain fuel his determination as they tore through the scrubby trees and headed for Brad's house.

No more. No more of this. My girls aren't going to grow up in a world where this can happen, not if I have any say in it.

So much had already happened, and this was only the beginning of their fight. There were still people working with the S.T.A.R.S. he trusted, that they could count on, and he wasn't going to be caught off his guard twice. The next time Umbrella came knocking, maybe they wouldn't have to run. And if Rebecca and David could pull off the Maine operation, they'd have what they needed to take the company down, once and for all.

Umbrella had messed with the wrong people. Barry planned on being there when they figured that out.

Jill picked the lock expertly, using a bent safety pin and one of Rebecca's earrings to open the door to the small cottage. Rebecca had swept Barry off to the medicine cabinet, while Chris went searching for a shirt. David and Jill checked the small house thoroughly, David's satisfaction growing with each passing moment.

He couldn't have imagined a better hideout, and it was comforting to know that Barry and the two Alphas would have a safe spot to work from. The two-bedroom home shared a backyard with a security-conscious family; bright lights snapped on when David opened the back door, flooding the small lawn brilliantly—and from the sight of the neighbor's side, they definitely had a rather large dog somewhere on the premises. There were houses close on either side of the rental, and the front window looked out on an open schoolyard just across the street. There would be no cover for an approaching team.

The house was furnished simply, if untidily; it was obvious that the occupant had fled in a panic. Personal items and books were strewn randomly across the rooms, as if Vickers had been unable to decide what to take in his hurry to flee Raccoon City.

With what happened tonight, I can't say I blame him for running. . . .

Mr. Vickers had obviously been in the wrong line of work, but that didn't necessarily make him a coward.

57

Risking one's life on a day-to-day basis wasn't for everyone—and considering the recent developments, it was wisest for someone like Vickers to remove himself from the situation. They could have used the help, but from what little Barry had told him, the Alpha pilot wasn't someone they wanted to work with. Even if he didn't get himself killed, he'd lost the trust of his teammates, and nothing could be worse when it came to crisis situations.

David sat in the dark, cramped living room on a rather hideous green couch, collecting his exhausted thoughts as Jill dug through the kitchen. He'd found a blank pad of paper and a pen, and had already scribbled down the names and home numbers of his team and various contacts, as well as Brad's phone number to take with him. He gazed blankly around the shadowed room, fighting off the adrenaline slump that so often followed battle. He didn't want to forget anything important, any detail that needed to be discussed before he and Rebecca left. If they wanted to make their plane, Barry, Jill, and Chris would have to deal with the aftermath of the attack on their own.

—the S.T.A.R.S., Trent's poem, objectives and contacts—

It was hard to focus after such a draining experience, and it didn't help matters that he'd been tired to begin with. He hadn't slept well in days, and thinking of all that lay ahead of them only made concentration harder. Rebecca's information about Dr. Griffith was disconcerting, to say the least, and though he was no less determined to carry out the Caliban Cove operation, it was just one more concern to add to a seemingly endless list.

Chris walked into the room wearing a faded blue sweatshirt with the sleeves cut off and fell into a chair across from David, his face hidden in shadow. After a moment, he leaned forward, enough light filtering through the closed blinds so that David could see his expression. The younger man's gaze was tired, thoughtful—and apologetic.

"Look, David . . . the last couple of weeks have been rough on all of us, you know? Waiting to see what Umbrella was gonna do, the suspension, feeling like our friends died for nothing . . ." Chris stopped himself, then started again. "I just wanted to say I'm sorry if we got off on the wrong foot earlier, and I'm glad you're on our side. I shouldn't have been such an asshole about it."

David was surprised and impressed by the sincerity behind the words; when he was in his twenties, he would've rather had his fingernails pulled out than display any emotion—except anger, of course. He'd had no trouble expressing anger.

Yet another legacy from dear old Dad. . . .

"I don't think you have anything to be sorry for," David said softly. "Your concerns are more than justified. I—I've been under a bit of strain myself, and I didn't mean to come across as domineering. The S.T.A.R.S. are—that is, they mean a lot to me, and I want us . . . I want for them to be *whole* again. . . ."

Jill walked in from the kitchen, saving David from

continuing with his fumbling speech. Much to his relief, Chris seemed to understand; he met David's gaze evenly, nodding, as if to say that the air had been cleared between them. David sighed inwardly, wondering if he'd ever be able to overcome his awkwardness with expressing emotions.

He'd done a lot of thinking since Barry had first called, about himself and his almost obsessive anger over the S.T.A.R.S. betrayal—and had come to the unsettling realization that he wasn't happy with the way his life was turning out. He'd thrown himself into his career in an effort to avoid dealing with a dysfunctional childhood, something he'd always known—but now, facing Umbrella and the treachery of an organization that he considered his family, he'd been forced to really think about the implications of his choice. It had made him an excellent soldier, but he didn't have any close friends or attachments . . . and having his "family" taken away had come as a cruel wake up to the fact that he had based his life on running from human contact.

Brilliant for me to have figured it out this late in the game. I suppose I should thank Umbrella for that much; if they don't kill me, they'll at least have managed to send me into therapy.

Jill had brought out a pitcher of water and several mismatched glasses which she passed around as Barry and Rebecca joined them. Barry wore a clean bandage on his arm and seemed pale in the dim light, certainly shaken by their discovery of Captain Shannon. David felt bad about killing Shannon, though he'd reconciled himself long ago to the realities of combat; in a war, people died. The captain had made his choice, and it had been the wrong one.

They drank in silence, the four Raccoon S.T.A.R.S. (*ex*-S.T.A.R.S., he reminded himself) pensive and somber, perhaps aware of the ticking clock. He and Rebecca would have to leave in a few moments. There was a convenience store a block away where they could telephone for a cab. David wished he could think of something encouraging to say, but the truth was the truth: they were going on a dangerous mission, and there were no guarantees that any of them would survive to meet again.

"Have you thought about what you'll tell the local police?" David asked finally.

Barry shrugged. "We won't have to lie much, anyway. The three of us were at my place, a buncha guys broke in and tried to shoot us. We ran."

"Irons will probably try to play it off as a botched burglary," Chris sneered. "If he's in this as deep as I think he is, he won't want to call attention to anything Umbrella's doing."

"Just be careful not to mention actually seeing any bodies," David said. "They may have had time to clean up. And you should say that you were chased into the park. It would explain your leaving the scene, as well as Captain Shannon's body—"

Barry smiled tiredly. "We'll handle it. And I'm going to make some calls first thing tomorrow, get us some backup. You just worry about your end, okay?"

David nodded and stood up, as did Chris. David

shook hands all around and then turned to Rebecca, uncomfortably aware that he was taking her from her teammates and trusted friends. The girl looked at the others in turn with a thoughtful expression—and then grinned suddenly, an unaffected and purely wicked smile.

"Sure you guys can hold down the fort for a couple of days? I hate to think of you flailing around all directionless while me and David go clean up this Umbrella thing."

"We'll try to limp along without you," Chris shot back, smiling. "Won't be easy, what with you having the brain and all. . . ."

Rebecca punched him lightly on the shoulder. "I'll send you a postcard with instructions."

She nodded at Barry. "Take care of your arm. Keep it clean and dry, and if you spike a fever or get dizzy, get to a doctor ASAP."

Barry smiled. "Yes, ma'am."

Jill embraced her lightly. "Give 'em hell, Becca."

Rebecca nodded. "You, too. Good luck with Irons."

She turned to David, still smiling. "Shall we?"

They walked to the front door together, David wondering at the girl's easy demeanor. They'd just barely survived a serious attack, carried out by people who'd probably trained her, and she was leaving with a man she hardly knew to embark on a life-threatening mission. She was either putting on an act or was amazingly optimistic—and if she was faking the casual bravado, she deserved an award.

He watched her carefully as they stepped out into

the small, unkempt yard of Brad Vickers's house, and saw her smile fade, quickly replaced by a look of vague sadness—and beyond that, the same kind of focused intensity that she'd had when she'd told them about Dr. Griffith and his research. Whatever she was thinking, he could see in that look that she was perfectly aware of the risks, but that she refused to be cowed by them.

The perfect definition of bravery. . . . David was satisfied with his decision to enlist Rebecca Chambers for the operation. She was smart, professional, and committed, as superior in her field of study as the rest of his team members were in theirs.

He could only hope that their combined skills would be enough to get them in and out of Caliban Cove in one piece, bringing with them proof of Umbrella's experiments—an objective that would lead to the ruin of the company that had corrupted the S.T.A.R.S., and perhaps let him sleep peacefully again.

David nodded, and the two of them set off to make the call.

After rereading the information on Caliban Cove, Rebecca folded the papers and carefully tucked them into the overnight bag under David's seat. He'd bought three bags at the airport, one for the weapons, currently in cargo, the others to carry on so they wouldn't attract attention. Rebecca wished they'd thought to buy some snacks while they were at it. She hadn't eaten since lunch, and the packet of nuts she'd swallowed after takeoff wasn't cutting it.

She reached up to switch off the reading light and then settled back in her seat, trying to let the smooth hum of the 747 engines lull her into a doze. Most of the other passengers on the half-full plane were asleep; the dim "night" lights and the steady drone of the engines had already worked for David. But even as drained as she felt by the evening's events, she gave up the effort after a minute or two. There was too much to think about, and she knew that she wouldn't be able to sleep without at least sorting through some of it.

I feel like I'm dreaming already anyway; this is just another weird tangent, a subplot that came out of left field. . . .

In the past three months, she'd graduated college, gone through S.T.A.R.S. Bravo training, and moved to her first apartment in a new city—only to end up one of the five survivors of a man-made disaster involving biological weapons and a corporate conspiracy. In the past three *hours,* her life had taken yet another totally unexpected turn. She thought about what she'd wished for earlier, a chance to get out of Raccoon City and study the T-Virus; the irony of the situation wasn't lost on her, but she wasn't so sure she liked the circumstances.

She rolled her head to the side and looked at David, crashed out in the window seat, dark circles of exhaustion beneath his closed lids. After briefly filling her in on a few details about the cove and outlining their schedule for the next day, he'd told her to try and take a nap ("have a lie down" had been his exact words) and then promptly taken his own advice—not falling asleep so much as lapsing into an instant coma.

He even sleeps efficiently, no tossing or turning . . . like he willed himself to get as much rest as possible in the time allowed.

He struck her as an extremely competent and intelligent man, if something of a loner; for as cool as he was under pressure, he seemed to freeze with small talk, leading her to wonder what kind of life he'd had. She was impressed with how quickly he'd come up with a plan to get them out of Barry's house, and was glad that he was leading the operation to Caliban Cove—though it was hard to think of him as a captain. He didn't really project authority, and didn't seem to want to, practically insisting that she call him David. Even when he'd stepped into a leadership role during the attack, it hadn't felt like he was giving them orders so much as offering instruction.

Maybe it's just the accent. Everything he says sounds polite. . . .

He frowned in his sleep, his eyes flickering through uneasy dreams. After a few seconds, he let out a soft, child-like moan of distress. Rebecca briefly considered waking him up, but already he seemed to have got past whatever troubled him, his brow smoothing. Suddenly feeling like she was invading his privacy, Rebecca looked away.

Dreaming about the attack, maybe. About having to kill someone he knew. . . .

She wondered if she'd be haunted by the image of the man she'd shot, the shadowy figure that had crumpled to the ground next to Barry's house. She was still waiting for the guilt to hit her—and thinking about it, she was surprised to find that her mind wasn't racing to rationalize the matter. She'd shot somebody, he could very well be dead—and all she felt was relief that she'd stopped him from killing her or anyone else on the team.

Rebecca closed her eyes, taking a deep breath of the cool, pressurized air hissing through the cabin. She could smell the musky odor of dried sweat on her skin, and decided that taking a shower was first priority when they hit the hotel. David didn't want to risk going back to his house on the off chance that someone on the strike force had recognized him, so they were going to grab a couple of rooms near the airport somewhere after they changed planes. The operation briefing was set for noon at the home of one of the other three team members, an Alpha forensics expert named Karen Driver. David had mentioned that Karen could probably lend her some clean clothes, though he'd actually blushed while saying it. He was a quirky one, all right. . . .

 . . . *and after the briefing, we get our equipment and go in, just like that.*

The thought knotted her stomach and sent a chill through her, telling her the real reason she wasn't able to sleep. Only two weeks after the Umbrella nightmare in Raccoon City, she was facing the same nightmare again. At least this time, she had some idea of what they'd be getting themselves into, and the plan was to get out of the facility without ever facing the T-Virus creatures—but the memory of Umbrella's Tyrant monster was still fresh in her mind, the massive, patchwork body and killing claw of the thing they'd seen on the estate. And the thought of what someone like Nicolas Griffith might have come up with using the virus . . .

Rebecca decided that she'd thought enough, she had to get some sleep. She cleared her mind as best she could and focused on her breathing, slowing it down, counting backward in her mind from one hundred. The meditation technique had never failed her before, though she didn't think it would work this time. . . .

. . . *ninety-nine, ninety-eight, Dr. Griffith, David, S.T.A.R.S., Caliban* . . .

Before she reached ninety, she was deeply asleep, dreaming of moving shadows that no light had cast.

FIVE

AS HE DID MOST MORNINGS SINCE BEGIN-
ning the experiment, Nicolas Griffith sat on the open
platform at the top of the lighthouse and watched the
sun rise over the sea. It was an awesome spectacle,
from beginning to end. First the black waves shading
to gray as the sky lightened, the craggy rocks that
lined his cove slowly taking form in the misty winds
that swept off the water. As the radiant star peered
over the side of the world, its first hesitant rays
stained the ocean a deep azure blue, painting the
pastel horizon with promises of renewal and a gentle,
nurturing acceptance of all that it touched.

It was a lie, of course. Within hours, the molten
giant would beat mercilessly against the shore, against
this half of the planet. Its early mildness was a

deception, a pretended ignorance of the seeping radiation and withering heat that would follow. . . .

. . . but no less spectacular for the lying. It can't be blamed for a lack of self-awareness, after all; it is what it is.

Griffith always watched until the sun cleared the curving horizon before getting on with his day. Although he appreciated the beauty of each glimmering dawn, it was the routine that appealed to him—not his, but that of the cosmos. Each sunrise was a statement of fact, speaking to an inevitable progression of time . . . and a reminder that the world spun eternally through its galactic paces, oblivious to the dreams of the self-important beings that scurried across its surface.

Beings such as myself, but for one very crucial difference: I know just how much my dreams are worth. . . .

As the swollen orb lifted itself from the sea, Griffith stood up and leaned against the platform railing, his thoughts turning to the day ahead. Having finally finished the blood work on the Leviathan series, he was ready to work more extensively with the doctors. All three had responded well to the change, and the rate of cellular deterioration had fallen considerably since he'd started with the enzyme injections. It was time to concentrate on their situational behavior, the final stage of the experiment. Within the week, he'd be ready to expand beyond the confines of the facility.

Expansion. A cleansing.

A crisp, saline wind ruffled his gray hair, the hungry cries of coasting gulls finally spurring him to action. The Trisquads had to be brought in before the scavenging birds moved inland. Several of the units had already been horribly scarred, and he didn't want to risk any more of them until he was finished. Once they lost their eyes, they were useless on patrol.

Still, it's been so long . . . no one's coming. If Dr. Ammon had succeeded, they'd have sent someone by now. Too bad, really; he's probably still waiting. . . .

The thought was an uncomfortable one, conjuring hazy images of redness and heat, of prone bodies in the manic summer sun and later, the thunder of waves in the dark. He promptly buried the visions, reminding himself that it was in the past. Besides, he'd only done what was necessary.

Griffith walked back inside, smoothing his wind-blown hair as he moved down the spiral staircase. His shoes clattered against the metal steps, creating a pleasant echo effect in the tall chamber. Having the facility to himself made everything pleasant, and he'd come to enjoy the little things—eating what he wanted when he wanted, working his own hours, his mornings atop the lighthouse. Before, he'd been crowded, forced to adhere to schedules that seemed designed to undercut creativity. Meal times, work times, sleep times . . . how could a man breathe, think, flourish in such conditions? He'd suffered for so long, sat through endless meetings listening to the small-minded drivel of his "colleagues" as they'd raved over Birkin's T-Virus. They'd slaved to come up with the Trisquads for Umbrella and had been deliriously happy with the results, apparently forgetting their failure with the Ma7s. They were unable to see past their own arrogance to a bigger picture. . . .

As if the Trisquads are anything more than bodies with guns. Useful as guards, but hardly brilliant. Hardly important.

Although he'd worked not to let it go to his head, Griffith allowed himself a single moment of pride as he reached the bottom of the stairs and started for the exit. He'd seen the T-Virus for what it really was—a crude but effective platform for something far greater. He'd isolated the proteins, reorganized the nucleocapsid's envelope to allow for variables in infective capacity, and created an answer, *the* answer to the blight that the human race had become. A solution without violence or suffering.

Smiling, he stepped through the door into the cool shadow of the lighthouse, the crash of breaking waves at his back as he walked toward the dormitory building. He'd already synthesized an airborne, and had enough of it to infect most of North America. As the virus spread, evolution would take its rightful place, the weak of spirit falling beneath those of truer instincts. And when it was over, the sun would rise over a very different world, inhabited by peaceful people of character and will.

Take away a man's ability to choose, his mind becomes free, a blank, clean slate. With training, he becomes a pet; without, he becomes an animal, as harmless and serenely simple as a mouse. Cover the

*world with such animals, and only the strong sur-
vive. . . .*

He stepped into the dorm's rec room and turned on
the lights, still smiling. His doctors were right where
he'd left them, sitting at the meeting table, eyes
closed. Ideally, he'd run through the tests with un-
trained subjects, but the three men would have to
suffice. They'd been infected with the strain he would
release, and were closest to what the world would
become in a few days.

My pets. My children.

Besides the research laboratory, the cove facility
was designed to train bio-weapons like the Trisquads
or Ma7s—but also to measure use of logic in the
humanoid subjects. In the bunkers there were a number of items he could use, from the simplest of peg
tests to complex puzzles for those subjects capable of
higher functioning. He doubted his doctors would be
able to manage even the red series, but watching their
reactions would provide valuable insight, particularly
the tests where there was a pressure factor.

*They think, but can't make decisions. They function,
but not without input. How will they fare, without my
guiding hand?*

As he approached the table, Dr. Athens opened his
eyes, perhaps to see if there was a threat coming. Of
the three, Tom Athens was the strongest, the most
likely to survive on his own; he'd been one of the behavior specialists. In fact, he'd come up with the
three-unit team idea, the Trisquad, insisting that the

infected units would work more efficiently in small groups. He'd been right.

Doctors Thurman and Kinneson remained still— and Griffith noticed a foul smell coming from one of them. Scowling, he looked down, his suspicion confirmed by the wetness on Dr. Thurman's pants.

He shit himself. Again.

Griffith felt a sudden, almost overwhelming pity for Thurman, but it was quickly replaced by irritated disgust. Thurman had been an idiot before, a decent enough biologist but as ridiculously narrow-minded as the rest of them. He'd grown most of the Ma7s himself, and when they turned out to be uncontrollable, he laid blame on everyone but himself. If anyone deserved to wallow in his own filth, it was Louis Thurman. It was just too bad that the good doctor wasn't capable of understanding how repulsively pathetic he'd become.

Without me, he wouldn't have lasted a day.

Griffith sighed, stepping back from the table. "Good morning, gentlemen," he said.

In unison, the three men turned their heads to look at him, their eyes as blank as their faces. As different as they were physically, the slackness of their features and slow, vapid gazes made them look like brothers.

"It seems that Dr. Thurman has evacuated his bowels," Griffith said. "He's sitting in feces. That's funny."

All three of them grinned widely. Dr. Kinneson actually chuckled. He'd been the last to be infected, so had suffered the least tissue deterioration. Given the proper instructions, Alan could probably still pass for human.

Griffith pulled the police whistle out of his pocket and put it on the table in front of Athens. "Dr. Athens, recall the Trisquads from duty. Tend to their physical needs and send them to the cold room. When you've finished, go to the cafeteria and wait."

Athens picked up the whistle as he stood, then walked out of the room, down the hall toward the dormitory's other entrance. The whistle would deactivate the teams and call them in. There were four Trisquads, twelve soldiers in all. They'd be roaming the woods along the fence, or moving stealthily around the bunkers, having been trained to stay away from the northeast area of the compound, the lighthouse, and dorm. Griffith had to admit, they were quite effective at their purpose. Umbrella had wanted soldiers that would kill without mercy, and fight until they were literally blown to pieces. The T-Virus had been good for that much, and since they'd sped up the amplification time, they'd been able to turn out subjects in hours, rather than days. Once trained with weapons, the Trisquads had become killing machines—although with the recent heat wave, he didn't know how much longer they'd be viable. . . .

Griffith turned his attention to Dr. Thurman, still grinning and stinking like some bloated infant. He even looked like a baby, pudgy and bald, his smile as innocent and guileless as a child's.

"Dr. Thurman, go to your room and remove your

clothes. Shower and dress in clean clothes, then go to the caves and feed the Ma7s. When you've finished, go to the cafeteria and wait."

Thurman stood up, and Griffith saw that the padded chair was wet and stained.

Christ.

"Take the chair with you," Griffith said, sighing. "Leave it in your room."

After he'd gone, Griffith sat down across from Alan, suddenly feeling tired. The anticipatory pride he'd felt only moments before was gone, leaving a cold emptiness in its place.

My children. My creation. . . .

The virus was so beautiful, so perfectly engineered that the first time he'd seen it, he'd wept. Months of private research, of picking apart the T-Virus and isolating effect, culminating in that first micrograph . . . while the others had been gloating over their war toys, he'd found the true path to a new beginning.

And do they appreciate what I've done? Do any of them know how crucial this is? Crapping himself like a disgusting child, like a monkey, disgracing my work, my life. . . .

Griffith looked at Alan Kinneson, studying his handsome features, his expressionless eyes. Dr. Kinneson stared back, waiting to be told what to do. He'd been a neurologist once. There were pictures in his room of his wife and baby, a little boy with a bright, beautiful smile. . . .

Griffith's sanity shuddered suddenly, a terrible,

rending twist that made him dizzy, a thousand voices screaming unintelligibly through the cracks of reality. For just a second, he felt as if he was losing his mind.

How many will just starve to death, sitting in puddles of filth, waiting? Millions? Billions?

"What if I'm wrong?" Griffith whispered. "Alan, tell me I'm not wrong, that I'm doing this for the right reasons. . . ."

"You're not wrong," Dr. Kinneson said calmly. "You're doing this for the right reasons."

Griffith stared at him. "Tell me your wife's a whore."

"My wife's a whore," Dr. Kinneson said. No pause. No doubt.

Griffith smiled, and the fear melted away.

Look what I've accomplished. It's a gift, my creation, a gift to the world. A chance for man to become strong again, a peaceful death for all the Louis Thurmans in existence, better than they deserve. . . .

He'd been working too hard, tiring himself, and the strain was getting to him. He was only human, after all . . . but he couldn't afford to let the stress of his body affect his mind again. There would be no more tests. He'd spend the day getting ready instead, preparing himself for the cleansing.

Tomorrow at sunrise Dr. Griffith would give his gift to the wind.

Six

KAREN DRIVER WAS A TALL, LANKY WOMAN in her early thirties, with short blond hair and a serious, businesslike demeanor. Her small home was spotlessly kept and almost antiseptically clean. The clothes she'd picked out for Rebecca were utilitarian and perfectly folded: a dark green T-shirt and crisp matching pants, black cotton socks and underwear. Even her bathroom seemed to reflect her personality; the white walls were lined with shelves, each neatly organized according to purpose.

Scratch a forensics scientist, find an obsessive-compulsive. . . .

Rebecca immediately felt guilty for thinking it. Karen had been welcoming enough, even friendly in a brusque way. Maybe she just hated clutter.

Rebecca sat on the edge of the toilet and cuffed the

overlong pants around her ankles, relieved to be out of her old clothes and feeling surprisingly clear-headed after a night of broken sleep. David had rented a car at the airport, and in the early hours of the morning, they'd found a cheap motel and staggered into their separate rooms, Rebecca too exhausted to do more than take off her shoes before crawling into bed. She woke just before ten, took a shower and had been waiting nervously when David knocked at her door.

Rebecca heard the front door open and close, new voices floating through the living room. She slipped on her high tops and laced them quickly, feeling her anxiety level jump a notch. The team was assembled. They were that much closer to going in, and though she'd thought of little else since waking up, the realization continued to come as a kind of shock. Umbrella's surprise attack on Barry's house already seemed like it had happened in another lifetime, though it had been only hours ago. . . .

. . . *and hours from now, this will all be over. It's what's gonna happen in between that worries me. David and his team weren't there, they didn't see the dogs, the snakes, those unnatural creatures in the tunnels . . . or Tyrant.*

Rebecca shook the images away as she stood up, scooping her dirty clothes off the floor and stuffing them into the empty bag that she'd carried on the plane. There was no reason to assume that the Caliban Cove facility would be the same, and worrying about it wouldn't change anything. She paused in front of the mirror, studying the tense features of the young woman she saw there, and then walked to the door.

She headed for the living room, past the sparkling kitchen and around a corner in the hall. She heard David's lilting voice, apparently summing up the events of the night before.

". . . said he'd ring some of the others first thing this morning. Another of the team has a contact in the FBI to use as a go-between and to initiate an investigation when we have proof. They'll be waiting to hear from us when we've completed today's operation—"

He broke off as Rebecca walked into the room, and all eyes turned to her. Karen had pulled a few extra chairs into the room and sat in one of them next to a low, glass topped coffee table. There were two men sitting on the couch, across from where David stood.

David smiled at her as both men got up, stepping forward to be introduced.

"Rebecca, this is Steve Lopez. Steve is our resident computer genius and our best marksman—"

Steve grinned, an aw-shucks smile that suited his boyish features perfectly as he shook her hand, his teeth white against his natural deep-tan coloring. He had dark, quick eyes and black hair, and was only a few inches taller than her.

Not much older, either. . . .

His gaze was friendly and direct, and in spite of the circumstances, Rebecca found herself wishing that she'd at least run a brush through her hair before coming out of the bathroom. Simply put, he was hot.

"—and this is John Andrews, our communications specialist and field scout."

John's skin was a deep mahogany brown and he didn't have a beard, but he reminded her of Barry nonetheless. He was massively built, his six-foot frame bulging with tightly packed muscle. He grinned brightly at her, his smile dazzling white.

"This is Rebecca Chambers, biochemist and field medic for the Raccoon City S.T.A.R.S.," David said.

John let go of her hand, still smiling. "Biochemist? Damn, how old are you?"

Rebecca smiled back, catching the glint of humor in his eyes. "Eighteen. And three-quarters."

John laughed, a deep, throaty chuckle as he sat back down. He glanced at Steve, then back at her.

"You better watch out for Lopez, then," he said, then dropped his voice to a mock whisper. "He just turned twenty-two. And he's single."

"Knock it off," Steve growled, his cheeks flushing. He looked at her, shaking his head.

"You'll have to excuse John. He thinks he's got a sense of humor and nobody can talk him out of it."

"Your mother thinks I'm funny," John shot back, and before Steve could respond, David held up a hand.

"That's enough," he said mildly. "We only have a few hours to organize if we mean to do this today. Let's get started, shall we?"

Steve and John's banter had been a welcome break from her tension, making her feel like one of the team almost instantly—but she was also glad to see the serious, intent looks on all of their faces as they turned their attention to David, watching him pull out Trent's information and lay it on the table. It was good to know that they were pros. . . .

. . . but will it matter? her mind whispered softly. *The S.T.A.R.S. in Raccoon were professionals, too. And even knowing the kind of research Umbrella's been doing, will it make any difference at all? What if the virus mutated and is still infectious? What if the place is crawling with Tyrants . . . or something worse?*

Rebecca had no answer for the insistent little whisper. She focused on David instead, silently telling herself that her anxieties wouldn't get in the way of her doing her job. And that her second mission wouldn't be her last.

For Rebecca's sake, David started the briefing as he would have with an entirely new team. As bright as she was, and with her previous experience at an Umbrella facility, he didn't want her to hold back for fear of speaking out of turn.

"Our objective is to get into the compound, collect evidence on Umbrella and their research, and get out again with as little trouble as possible. I'll go over every step thoroughly, and if any of you have questions or ideas about how to proceed, no matter how trifling, I want to hear them. Understood?"

There were nods all around. David continued, comfortable that his point was made.

"We've already discussed a few of the possibilities as to what may have happened, and you've all read the articles. I submit that we're dealing once again with some kind of accident. Umbrella's put a lot of effort into covering up the problem in Raccoon City, and while we could assume that they've been abducting or killing fishermen who've wandered across their territory, it seems unlikely that they'd want to draw that kind of attention to themselves."

"Why hasn't Umbrella sent anyone in to clean it up?" John asked.

David shook his head. "Who's to say they haven't? We may find that they've already cleared the site of evidence—in which case, we group together with the Raccoon people and our own contacts and start over."

Again, everyone nodded. He didn't bother stating the obvious, that the virus could still be contagious. They all knew that it was a possibility, though he planned to have Rebecca address the matter before the briefing was through.

David looked down at the map and sighed inwardly before moving on to the next point.

"Point of entry," he said. "If this were an open assault, we could go in by helicopter or just hop the fence. But if there are still people there and we trigger an alarm, it's over before we even start. Since we don't want to risk discovery, our best option is to go in by boat. We can use one of the rafts from the tanker operation last year."

Karen piped up, frowning slightly.

"Wouldn't they have an alarm for the pier?"

David touched the map, putting his finger just below the notched line of the fence, south of the compound. "Actually, I don't recommend using the pier at all. If we go in here, go past the pier—" He traced upward, running the length of the cove. "—we can get a look at the layout of the entire compound, and hide the raft in one of the caves beneath the lighthouse. According to what I read, there's a natural path from the base of the cliff to the lighthouse itself. If the path has been blocked, we'll backtrack and come up with an alternative route."

"Won't the raft attract attention if anyone's outside watching?" Rebecca asked.

David shook his head. The Exeter S.T.A.R.S. had used the rafts the previous summer to approach an oil tanker that had been hijacked by terrorists who had threatened to spill the cargo unless their demands were met. It had been a night operation.

"It's black, and has an underwater motor. If we go in just past dusk, we should be invisible. The other benefit to this approach is that if the facility looks— *unhealthy*, we can abort until a later time."

He waited as they thought it over, not wanting to rush them. They were good soldiers, his team, but this was a volunteer assignment. If any one of them had serious doubts, it was better to address them now. Besides which, he was open to other suggestions.

His gaze fell across Rebecca's youthful face, taking in the steady willingness of a good S.T.A.R.S. operative in the quick brown eyes, the thoughtful consideration of his plan. He was beginning to like her, for more than just her usefulness to the mission. There was a kind of matter-of-fact openness about her that appealed to him, particularly with all of his recent turmoil over emotional awkwardness. She seemed quite comfortable with herself. . . .

David pushed the thoughts aside, suddenly realizing how much stress he'd been under, how tired he continued to be; his focus was suffering for it.

Keep it together, man. This isn't the time to wander.

"On to specifics," he said. "Once we get inside, we move in a staggered line through the compound, sticking to shadows. John will take point with Karen at his back, scouting the area for the lab and looking for some idea as to what's happened. Steve and Rebecca will follow, and I'll bring up the rear. When we find the lab, we go in together. Rebecca will know what to look for in terms of materials, and if they have a computer system still running, Steve can get into the files. The rest of us will provide cover. Once we retrieve the information, we get back out the way we came."

He picked up the poem that Trent had given him, tapping it with his other hand. "One of Rebecca's teammates has already had dealings with Mr. Trent. She thinks that this might be relevant to what we need to find, so I want all of you to take another look before we go in. It may be important."

"So we can trust him?" Karen asked. "This Trent's okay?"

David frowned, not sure how to answer. "It seems that for whatever reason, he's on our side in all of this, yes," he said slowly. "And Rebecca recognized one of the names on the list as a man who has worked with viruses before. The information looks solid." It wasn't a straight answer, but it would have to do.

"Any idea on what the chances are that we'll contract the virus?" Steve asked quietly.

David tilted his head toward Rebecca. "If you could give us some insight about what we may see, perhaps a bit of background . . ."

She nodded, turning toward the rest of the team. "I can't tell you *exactly* what we're dealing with. When our team got kicked off the case, I lost access to the tissue and saliva samples, so I didn't get to run any tests. But from looking at the effects, it's pretty obvious that the T-Virus is a mutagen, altering the host's chromosome structure on a cellular level. It's an interspecies infective, capable of amplifying in plants, mammals, birds, reptiles, you name it. In some creatures, it promotes incredible growth; in all of them, violent behavior. From some of the reports we came across at the estate, I can tell you that it affects brain chemistry, at least in humans—inducing something like a schizophrenic psychosis through extremely high levels of D2 receptors. It also inhibits pain. The human victims we came across hardly reacted to gunshot wounds, and though they were decaying physically, they didn't seem to feel it. . . ."

The young chemist paused, perhaps remembering.

She suddenly looked much older than her years. "The spill at the estate looked like an airborne, but I don't think that's its designed or preferred form. The scientists were almost certainly injecting it in conjunction with genetic experimentation. And since none of us contracted it and it didn't spread, I don't think we have to worry about breathing it in.

"What we *do* have to watch for is contact with a host, and I mean *any* contact, I can't stress that enough—this thing is incredibly virulent once it enters the bloodstream, and even a single drop of blood from a host could hold hundreds of millions of virus particles. We'd need a fully equipped hot suite and a trained biohazard virologist to pin down its replication strategy for certain, but direct contact of any kind should be avoided at all costs. With any luck, they'll have died by now . . . or at least deteriorated past mobility. The humans, anyway."

There was a moment of strained silence as they all considered the implications of what she'd told them. David could see that they were shaken, and felt a bit shaken himself. Knowing that the virus was toxic wasn't the same thing as actually hearing the specifics.

My God, what were those people thinking? How could they live with themselves, deliberately infecting anything *with something like that?*

On the tail of that thought, another occurred to him: how would he live with himself if one of his team contracted the virus? He'd led missions before in which people under his command had been hurt—

and twice, before he made captain, he'd been on operations in which S.T.A.R.S. had been killed. But taking a team into an area on his own initiative, where a silent, terrible disease could infect them, where they could die at the claws of some inhuman monster . . .

. . . it would be on my head. This isn't an authorized mission, the responsibility stops with me. Can I truly ask them to do this?

"Well, it pretty much sounds like a shit job," John said finally. "And if we wanna get there on time, we better head out soon." He smiled at David, an uncharacteristically subdued one but a smile all the same. "You know me, I love a good fight. And somebody's gotta stop these assholes from spreading this stuff around, right?"

Steve and Karen were both nodding, their faces as set and determined as John's, and even knowing what they would encounter, Rebecca had made her decision back in Raccoon. David felt a sudden rush of emotion for all of them, a strange, uncomfortable mix of pride and fear and warmth that he wasn't sure what to do with.

After a few seconds of uncertain silence, he nodded briskly, glancing at his watch. It would take them a few hours to get to the launch site.

"Right," he said. "We'd best get to storage and load up. We can go through the rest of it on our way."

As they stood to leave, David reminded himself that they were doing this because it was necessary, that each of them had made up their own mind to participate in the dangerous operation. They knew the risks. And he also knew that if anything went wrong, that knowledge would be cold comfort indeed.

Karen sat in the back of the van and loaded clips, the words of the mysterious message repeating through her thoughts as she thumbed the nine-millimeter rounds into each magazine.

. . . Ammon's message received/blue series/enter answer for key/letters and numbers reverse/time rainbow/don't count/blue to access.

She finished another clip and set it aside with the others, absently wiping her oily fingers on the leg of her pants before picking up the next. A welcome breeze whispered through the muggy van, smelling of salt and summer-warmed sea. They'd pulled off the road south of the cove, finding a clear patch to set up not a quarter mile from the water's edge. Outside, the sun was setting, casting long shadows across the dusty ground. The not-so-distant sound of soft waves against the shore was soothing, a white noise background to the low voices of the others as they worked. Steve and David were prepping the raft, while John checked out the motor. Rebecca was assembling a medical kit from the supplies they'd "borrowed" out of the S.T.A.R.S. equipment warehouse.

. . . the letters and numbers . . . a code? Does it

relate to time? Does counting relate to the sum of the lines, or to something else?

Her mind worked the riddle relentlessly, gnawing at the words the way a dog worries a bone. What did it mean? Were the lines connected to a single concept, or did each represent a separate aspect of a bigger puzzle? Had Ammon sent the message, and if he worked for Umbrella, why?

She finished the last clip and reached for a waterproof carryall, refocusing herself to the task at hand. She knew that her thoughts would return to the strange little poem as soon as she'd completed her assigned detail. It was the way her mind worked; she just couldn't relax when presented with an ambiguity. There was always an answer, always, and finding it was just a matter of concentration, of taking the right steps in the right order.

The semi-automatics were cleaned and ready, laying in a neat line next to the checked radio gear on the floor of the van. They weren't taking any weapons besides the S.T.A.R.S.-issued Berettas, David insisting that they needed to travel light. Although Karen agreed, she was sorry they wouldn't be bringing in the assault rifles, which were equipped with night scopes. After hearing more of the details about the zombie-like creatures on their ride, she didn't know how comfortable she felt with just a handgun and a halogen flashlight.

Admit it. You're worried about this one, and have been since David broke the news. The facts are all out of order, the pieces don't fit the way they're supposed to.

It was ironic that the reasons compelling her to crack this mystery were the same ones that made her so uneasy: Trent, the S.T.A.R.S.'s apparent collusion with Umbrella, the possibility of a biohazardous incident in her home state. Who had been bribed? What had happened at Caliban Cove? What would they uncover? What did the poem mean?

Not enough data. Not yet.

She'd always prided herself on her lack of imagination, on her ability to find the truth based on empirical evidence rather than wild, unsubstantiated intuition. It was the key to success in her field, and though she was aware that she sometimes came across as overly clinical—even cold—she accepted who she was, embracing the kind of peace that was found in knowing all of the facts. Whether it was examining blood spray patterns or measuring angles on an entry wound, there was a deep satisfaction for her in solving puzzles, in finding out not only *why*, but *how*. The unanswered questions about Caliban Cove were an affront to her careful thought processes. They went against her grain, smudging her very ordered sense of reality—and she knew that she wouldn't find relief until those questions were put to rest.

She was finished with the weapons. She should check the utility belts again, make sure everything was locked down and ready, and then see if David had anything else for her to do. . . .

Karen hesitated, feeling a trickle of warm sweat slide down her back. No one was within sight of the open back door, and she'd already double-checked every flap and pocket on every belt. With a sudden rush of something like guilt, she reached into her vest pocket and pulled out her secret, comforted by the familiar weight of it in her hand.

God, if the guys knew, I'd never hear the end of it.

It had been given to her by her father, a remnant from his service in WWII and one of the few items she had to remember him by—an ancient anti-personnel shrapnel grenade, called a *pineapple* because of its crosshatched exterior. Carrying it was one of her few unpractical idiosyncrasies, one that made her feel a little silly. She'd worked hard to present herself as a thoroughly rational, intelligent woman, not prone to emotional sentimentality—and in most respects, that was true. But the grenade was her rabbit's foot, and she never went on a mission without it. Besides, she had half convinced herself that it might come in handy one day. . . .

Yeah, keep telling yourself that. The S.T.A.R.S. have digitized anti-personnel grenades with timers, even flash-bangs with computer chips. The pin on this relic probably couldn't be wrenched out with pliers—

"Karen, do you need any help?"

Startled, Karen looked up and into Rebecca's earnest young features, the girl leaning into the back of the van. Her quick gaze fell to the grenade, her eyes lighting up with sudden curiosity.

"I thought we weren't taking any explosives . . . hey, is that a pineapple grenade? I've never actually seen one. Is it live?"

Karen quickly looked around, afraid that one of the team had overheard—then grinned sheepishly at the young biochemist, embarrassed by her own embarrassment.

It's not like I got caught masturbating, for chrissake; she doesn't know me, why the hell would she care if I'm superstitious?

"Shh! They'll hear us. Come here a sec," she said, and Rebecca obediently crawled into the van, a conspiratorial half-smile blooming on her face. In spite of herself, Karen was absurdly pleased by the young biochemist's discovery. In the seven years she'd been with the S.T.A.R.S., no one had ever found out. And she'd taken an instant liking to the girl.

"It *is* a pineapple, and we're not taking explosives in. You can't tell anyone, okay? I carry it for good luck."

Rebecca raised her eyebrows. "You carry a live grenade around for luck?"

Karen nodded, looking at her seriously. "Yes, and if John or Steve found out, they'd ride me ragged. I know it's dumb, but it's kind of a secret."

"I don't think it's dumb. My friend Jill has a lucky hat. . . ." Rebecca reached up and touched her headband, a tied red bandana beneath mousy bangs. ". . . and I've been wearing this for a couple of weeks practically. I was wearing it when we went into the Spencer facility."

Her young face clouded slightly, and then she was smiling again, her light brown gaze direct and sincere. "I won't say a word."

Karen decided that she definitely liked her. She tucked the grenade back in her vest, nodding at the girl. "I appreciate that. So, are we ready out there?"

Tiny lines of nervous strain appeared on Rebecca's face. "Yeah, pretty much. John wants to run another check with the headsets, but other than that, everything's done."

Karen nodded again, wishing she could say something to ease the girl's fear. There wasn't anything *to* say. Rebecca had dealt with Umbrella before, and any words that Karen might mouth would be hollow ones, might even seem patronizing. She felt some anxiety herself, she'd be a fool not to—but fear wasn't a state that she wore often or well. As with most missions, the overriding feeling she experienced was anticipation, a kind of cerebral hunger for the truth.

"Go ahead and hand out the weapons, I'll get the rest," Karen said finally. She could at least give her something to do.

Rebecca helped her unload the equipment as the sun dipped lower in the heavy summer sky. The winds off the water grew cooler and the first pale stars shimmered into view over the Atlantic.

As twilight crept in, they moved down to the water in an uneasy silence, loading their weapons, stretching, staring out at the black waters that eddied and swirled with secrets of their own.

When the last of the daylight melted off the horizon, they were as ready as they were going to get. As John and David slipped the raft into the lapping darkness, Karen slipped on a black watchcap and patted the heavy lump inside her vest for luck, telling herself that she wouldn't need it.

The truth was waiting. It was time to find out what was really going on.

SEVEΠ

STEVE AND DAVID CLIMBED IN, EDGING TO the front of the six-man raft as Karen and Rebecca followed. John hopped in last, and at David's signal, started the motor with the push of a button; it was as silent as David had promised, only a faint hum that was almost lost in the sound of gently moving water.

"Let's move," David said quietly. Rebecca took a deep breath and let it out slowly as they started north, heading for the cove.

Nobody spoke as the shore slid by to their left, shadowy, jagged shapes in the pallid light of the rising moon, an immense and whispering void to their right.

Port and starboard, her mind noted randomly. *Bow and stern.*

She searched the blackness for a sign that marked the beginning of the private territory, but couldn't make out much. It was a lot darker than she'd expected, and colder. The chill she felt was compounded by the knowledge that beneath them lay an infinite and alien world, teeming with cold-blooded life.

Rebecca saw a flash of soft light as David raised a pair of NV binoculars to watch for movement on the shore. The infrared illuminator's glow spilled across his face for an instant before he adjusted their position, making his features strange and craggy.

Now that they were actually doing it, actually on their way, she felt better than she had all day. Not relaxed, by any means—the dread was still there, the fear of the unknown and for what they might encounter—but the feelings of helplessness, the mind-numbing anxiety she'd lived with since the incident in Raccoon, had eased, giving way to hope.

We're doing something, taking the offensive instead of waiting for them to get to us—

"I see the fence," David said softly, his face a pale smudge in the bobbing dark.

We'll pass the dock next, maybe see the buildings as the land slopes up to the lighthouse, to the caves . . .

Water slopped at the raft, the sound of muted waves growing as the small craft rocked and shuddered. Rebecca felt her heart speed up. While she liked looking at the ocean, she wasn't all that thrilled to be out in it; as a kid, she'd seen *Jaws* one time too many.

She kept her focus on the shore, trying to judge how close they were, and felt as much as saw the land open up as the tiny raft slipped through the lapping waves.

Maybe twenty meters away, the towering shadows of trees gave way to a clearing. She could hear water dashing lightly against the rocky shore, sense flat, open space on both sides of them now. They had reached the compound.

"There's the dock," David said. "John, veer starboard, two o'clock."

Rebecca could just make out the faint, man-made shape of the pier ahead of them, a dark line shifting on the water. There was the hollow, lonely squeak of metal rubbing wood, the small dock raised and straining at its pilings. There were no boats that she could see.

As the pier slipped past, Rebecca squinted into the darkness beyond. She could just make out the blocky outline of a structure behind the floating wood, what had to be the boathouse or marina for the facility. She couldn't see any of the other buildings from Trent's map. There were six more besides the lighthouse, five of them spaced evenly along the cove, set into two lines that paralleled the shore—three in front, two behind. The sixth structure was directly in back of the lighthouse, and they were all hoping that it was the lab; they'd be able to get what they needed without going through the whole compound—

"Boathouse is wood, the others look like concrete. I don't—wait," David's whisper became urgent. "Somebody—two, three people, they just went behind one of the buildings."

Rebecca felt a strange relief flood through her, relief and disappointment and a sudden confusion. If there

were people, maybe the T-Virus hadn't been un-
leashed. But that meant that the buildings would be
occupied, the grounds patrolled, making a covert
operation impossible.

*Then why is it so dark? And why does it feel so dead
here, so empty?*

"Do we abort?" Karen whispered, and before David could respond, Steve gasped, a sharp intake of air
that froze Rebecca's blood, her thoughts fluttering
wildly in a spasm of primal fear.

"Three o'clock, big, oh Jesus it's *huge*—"

BAM!

The raft was hit, heaved up and over in a fountain
of churning blackness. Rebecca saw a flash of sky,
smelled cold and rotting slime—and was plunged,
splashing, into the turbulent dark waters of the sea.

Water enveloped him, the icy, stinging salt burning
David's eyes and nose as he flailed desperately, lost
and breathless.

—where is it—

He'd seen it, an immense and pebbled plain of flesh
surging up from the black at the second of impact.
The surface pulled at him and he kicked against the
dragging depths, terrified. His head broke through to
air and an ominous quiet.

—the team where's—

David whirled around, gasping, heard a spluttering
cough to his left.

"Get to shore," he panted, turning in a circle, trying

to find their position, to find the creature's, cursing himself for a fool.

Missing fishermen, haunted waters, stupid, stupid—

The raft was ten meters behind him, upside down, disturbed water splashing at its sides. The force of the attack had thrown them clear, actually knocking them closer to land. He saw two bobbing shapes, faces between him and the shore, heard more splashing as another joined them. He couldn't see the unnatural thing that had hit the raft but expected to feel the bite any second, the cold puncture of dagger teeth tearing him to pieces.

"Get to shore," he called again, his heart thundering, his legs heavy and vulnerable, kicking, obvious.

Can't go in, three, where's four?

"David—"

John's terrified shout, from beyond the floating raft.

"Here! John, this way, come this way, follow my voice!"

John started toward him as David tread water, propelling himself backward toward the rocky beach and shouting all the while. He saw the top of John's head appear, saw his arms pumping frantically through the murky water.

"—follow me, I'm over here, we have to get—"

A giant, pale shadow rose up smoothly behind the soldier, at least three meters across, rounded and dripping and impossible. Time jerked to a crawl, the events unfolding in front of him in a slow motion dream. David saw thick, tapering tentacles on either side near the top of the rising shadow, saw a rounded slash in the corpse-colored slickness—

—*not tentacles, feelers*—

—and realized that he was seeing the underbelly of a monstrous animal that couldn't possibly exist, a bottom feeder as big as a house. The black slash of its mouth hissed open, revealing clusters of peg-like, grinding teeth, each the size of a man's fist.

When it came down, John would be swallowed up by the massive jaws. Or crushed. Or plowed into the icy deep, a drowning meal for the creature.

In the instant it took him to absorb the facts, he was already screaming.

"Dive! Dive!"

Time skipped forward and the beast was falling forward, arching over, its long, thick serpent's body dwarfing the raft, its shadow enveloping the frantic swimmer. David caught a glimpse of bulbous, rolling eyes the size of beach balls—

—and it crashed down, sending explosive plumes of water high into the air, blotting out the stars in sheets of foaming spray. Before David could draw breath, a tremendous wave knocked into him, driving him violently backward through the bubbling darkness.

There was rushing movement, a sense of helpless speed as he struggled against the force that tore at his limbs, struggled to find air in the sweeping torrent. Kicking wildly, he surged upward through the liquid veil, felt cold air slap at his skin—and warm, human hands yanking at his shoulders. He inhaled convulsively as his boots scraped against rock and Karen's ragged voice spoke behind him.

"Got him—"

Staggering against the slimy rocks, David let himself be dragged backward until he found his balance and could turn around. Wet figures were reaching out, Steve and Rebecca—

Oh my God, John—

"I'm okay," David gasped, stumbling forward, his knees cracking numbly against larger rocks that his blurred gaze denied him from seeing. "John—does anyone see him?"

Nobody answered. He blinked away salt, reeling around to face the splashing darkness, the settling waves slapping at their feet.

"John—" he called, as loud as he dared, searching, seeing nothing at all. His heart was as cold as his body, as heavy as the sodden weight of his Kevlar vest.

—no life jackets, would've seen him by now—

He called again, hope dwindling. "John!"

A choking, strangled voice from the rocks to their left. "What?"

David sagged in relief, taking a deep breath as John's dripping figure staggered out of the shadows. Steve lunged forward, grabbing the taller man's arm and helping him lean against the rocks.

"I dove," John rasped out.

David turned and looked up, past the sliver of pebbled, boulder-strewn beach to the darkness of the compound. They were at the bottom of a short, angled drop, in plain sight. The shock of the monstrous fish—if it could be called that—was suddenly unimportant in the light of that realization. They were out of the water now.

Have they heard us? Seen? Won't make the caves now, can't stay here—

"The marina," he breathed, turning south, "quickly—"

The team stumbled past him, Karen taking the lead, the others following close. No one seemed seriously injured, a miracle all its own. David jogged after John, assessing the situation as his aching legs carried him through the rocky dark.

Get to cover, bar the door, regroup, get to the fence—

The ground rose steeply in front of them, the pier looming into view ahead. As they clambered up over rocks, David heard a muffled clatter of metal, saw Rebecca hugging the black, dripping shape of the ammo pack to her chest. He felt a wisp of new hope for their chances; if they could just make it inside, somewhere safe . . .

The building was ahead on their right, silent and dark, a closed door facing the wooden dock. There was no way to know if it was empty, and though barely ten meters away, the distance was open and flat, weathered planking, not even a pebble to block them from view.

No choice.

"Stay low," he whispered, and then they were crouching their way to the structure, Karen reaching the door first, pushing it open. No light spilled out, no alarm sounded. Steve and Rebecca piled in behind her, then John—then David, stumbling into the dark, closing the wooden door after him with a wet, cold shoulder.

"Stop where you are," he said softly, fumbling for the halogen torch on his belt. Besides the gulping breaths of his team, the room was still—but there was a horrid smell in the close air, a fading stench of something long dead. . . .

The thin beam of light cut through the black, revealing a large and mostly empty windowless room. Ropes and life preservers hung from wooden pegs, a workbench ran the length of one wall, a few saw horses, cluttered shelves—

—my God—

The light froze on the room's other door, directly across from the one they'd entered. The narrow beam played across the source of the smell, highlighting bare bone and a tattered, oily-stained lab coat. Dried strings of muscle dripped in streamers from a grinning face.

A corpse had been nailed to the door, one hand fixed in a welcoming wave. From the look, it had been dead for weeks.

Steve felt his gorge rise into his throat. He swallowed it down, looking away, but the grotesque image was already fixed in his mind—the eyeless face and peeling tissue, the carefully splayed fingers pinned into place. . . .

Jesus, is that some kind of a joke? Steve felt dizzy,

still out of breath from the nightmarish swim, the sloshing climb over the rocks, the horror of the Umbrella sea monster. The dried, sour smell of rot wasn't helping.

For a few seconds, nobody spoke. Then David cupped one hand over the light and started talking, his voice low but amazingly even.

"Check your belts and drop your clips. I want status, now, injuries then equipment. Take a deep breath, everyone. John?"

John's solemn voice rumbled through the shadows to Steve's left, accompanied by sounds of wet, fumbling movement. Karen and Rebecca were to his right, David still by the door.

"I got fish slime on me, but I'm okay. I've got my weapon but my light's gone. So are the radios."

"Rebecca?"

Her voice was wavering but quick. "I'm fine—uh, my weapon's here, and the flashlight, the med kit . . . oh, and I've got the ammo."

Steve checked himself out as she spoke, unholstering his Beretta and ejecting the wet mag, slipping it into a pocket. There was an empty spot on his belt where his light should have been.

"Steve?"

"Yeah, no injuries. Weapon but no light."

"Karen?"

"Same."

David's fingers shifted over the muted beam, allowing a shallow glow to spill into the room. "No one's hurt and we're still armed; things could be a lot worse. Rebecca, pass out the clips, please. The fence can't be more than fifty meters south from here, and there are enough trees for cover, provided no one has seen us yet. This operation is called, we're getting out of here."

Steve accepted three loaded magazines from Rebecca, nodding his thanks. He slapped one into the semi, chambering a round automatically.

Great, fine, let's blow. That insane creature nearly eating us, now Mr. Death dropping a casual wave, like he was put there to say hello. . . .

Steve wasn't easily frightened, but he knew a bad situation when he saw it. He admired the S.T.A.R.S. deeply, had wanted to go in on the operation to help make things right—but with their boat gone and the initial plan shot to shit, nailing Umbrella could wait.

David stepped closer to the decomposed figure, a look of disgust curling his features in the shadowy orange glow of the light. "Karen, Rebecca, come take a look at this. John, take Rebecca's torch, you and Steve see if you can find anything useful."

Rebecca handed her flashlight to John, who nodded at Steve. The two men walked to one end of the long workbench, the soft voices of the others carrying across the still air.

"The T-Virus didn't do this," Rebecca said. "Pattern of decay's all wrong. . . ."

Silence, then Karen spoke. "See that? David, give me the light for a sec—"

John hooded their flashlight with one large hand, playing the beam across the dirty planks of the counter. A broken coffee mug. A pile of greasy nuts and bolts on top of a laminated tide chart. An electric screwdriver, dusty and dented, a couple of bits on a stained rag.

Nothing, there's nothing here. We should get out before someone comes looking . . .

John opened a drawer and rummaged through it while Steve tried to make out what was on an overhead shelf. Behind them, Karen spoke again.

"He wasn't dead when they nailed him up, though I'd say he was close. Definitely unconscious. There's no smearing, suggesting he didn't struggle . . . and there are slide marks, here and here; I'd say he was shot by the back door and dragged over."

John had finished digging through the drawer and they moved on, boots squelching against the wood floor. A set of socket wrenches. A cheap radio. A crumpled paper bag next to a pencil nub.

Something snagged at Steve's thoughts and he stopped, looking at the paper bag. The pencil . . .

He picked up the crunched ball, smoothing out the wrinkles and turning it over. There were several lines written near the bottom, scrawled and jerky.

"Hey, we found something," John called quietly, shining the light on the writing as the others hurried over. Steve read it aloud, squinting at the faintly penciled words under the wobbling beam. There was no punctuation; he did his best to work out the pauses as he went.

". . . 'July 20. Food was drugged, I'm sick—I hid the material for you, sent data. Boats are sunk and he let the . . .'"

Steve frowned, unable to make out the word. *Tris . . . tri-squads?*

"'Boats are sunk and he let the Trisquads out—dark now, they'll come, I think he killed the rest—stop him—God knows what he means to do. Destroy the lab—find Krista, tell her I'm sorry, Lyle is sorry. I wish—'"

There was nothing more.

"Ammon's message," Karen said softly. "Lyle Ammon."

It didn't take a rocket scientist to figure out who was hanging on the door. The sagging, seeping Mr. Death had an identity now, for what it was worth. And the message that Trent had given David was so weird because the poor guy had apparently been doped up when he sent it.

"Nice to put a face to the name, huh?" John cracked, but not even he smiled. The desperate little note had an ominous ring to it, with or without the brutal murder to back it up.

What's a Trisquad? Who's "he"?

"Maybe we should look around a little more—" Rebecca began hesitantly, but David was shaking his head.

"I think it's best if we leave this for now. We'll—" He broke off as heavy, plodding footsteps sounded across the wood deck, just outside the door they'd come through. Everyone froze, listening. More than one set, and whoever they were, they were making no effort to hide their approach. They stopped at the door—and stayed there, no rattling knob, no crashing kick, no other sound. Waiting.

David circled one finger in the air, pointed to Karen and then to the other door, hung with the grisly remains of Lyle Ammon. The signal to move out, Karen first.

They edged toward the grinning corpse, Steve wincing at every shifting creak they created, breathing through his mouth to avoid inhaling the stench—

—and as Karen pushed the door open, the silence was shattered by the rattle of automatic fire, coming from in front of them, to the left—coming from the direction of their escape.

Eight

KAREN JUMPED BACK AS BULLETS CRACKED into the door. Chunks of rotten flesh spattered up from Ammon's body; the corpse danced and waved in a shuddering, jerking rhythm of macabre motion.

David snatched at the coat of the dead man and yanked, but the door was pinned open by the clattering fire—and whoever was shooting was coming closer, the explosive shots louder, the splinters of flesh and wood pelting them with greater force. They were trapped, both exits blocked.

Rebecca clutched her Beretta in one shaking hand, watching for a signal from David. He pointed roughly northwest, into the compound, shouting to be heard over the whining, spitting clatter of the automatic fire.

"Rebecca, other door! John, Karen, next building, secure! Steve, we cover! *Go!*"

As one, Steve and David leaped out and started to fire, the booming rounds punctuating the lighter hail of deadly ammo.

John and Karen charged out at a full run, were instantly swallowed up by the shadows. Rebecca spun and trained her weapon on the back door, her heart pounding in her throat. The walls trembled and shook.

"Die, Jesus, why won't they die?" Steve screamed behind her, a strain of disbelief and terror in his voice that made her blood run cold.

—zombies?

Without looking away from the rectangle of dark wood, Rebecca shouted as loud as she could, her voice cracking over the relentless spray of the automatics.

"Head shots! Aim for the head!"

There was no way to know if they'd heard her, the rifle or rifles kept pounding, approaching. Her thoughts raced to understand, images of the T-Virus victims flitting through her mind. They'd been mindless, slow, inhuman—

—and accidental, not on purpose—not with purpose—

"Rebecca, let's go!"

There was still the sound of an automatic rifle firing, but the boathouse no longer shook from the impact of its force. She shot a glance back, saw Steve still shooting at something, saw David motioning at her to move.

She sidled for the open door, catching a sickening, up-close look at the bullet-riddled corpse still hanging there. The head had caved in like a rotting pumpkin, teeth shattered, gummy flecks of tissue radiating out from behind the skull. The waving hand was no longer connected to the rotting arm, the radius and ulna blown away. It dangled there like some obscene decoration, beckoning . . .

Steve fired once more and the auto's clatter ceased. He raised the weapon, his eyes wide and shocked as he opened his mouth to say something—

—and the back door crashed open, bullets flying through the dark in a blaze of orange fire. David pushed her roughly through the front and she ran, the responding *crack* of nine-millimeter rounds resonating behind her.

—get to the building, get to cover—

She sprinted through the shadows, her wet shoes thumping across packed, rocky dirt, her searching gaze finding the outline of a massive, concrete block and the spindly trees that surrounded it in the darkness ahead.

"Here—"

She veered toward the call, saw John's muscular form silhouetted by pale starlight at the corner of the building. As she neared him, she saw the open door, Karen standing in the entry with her weapon trained back toward the boathouse. Bullets still sang through the shadows.

"Get in!" Karen shouted, stepping out of the way, and Rebecca ran past her, not slowing until she was inside. She fell into a table in the pitch black, cracking one hip painfully against the edge.

Turning, she saw Karen firing, heard John yelling, "Come on, come *on*—"

—and Steve pounded through the door, gasping. He pulled to a stop before crashing into her, one hand clutching his chest.

Rebecca moved to the door and grasped the cool thickness, her mind absently registering that the material was steel as David hurtled through, shouting.

"Karen, John!—"

Karen backed into the darkness, weapon still raised. There were three more sharp reports from a Beretta and then John slipped inside, his jaw clenched, his nostrils flaring.

Rebecca slammed the door, her fingers finding a deadbolt switch. The soft *snick* of the lock was barely audible against the ringing in her ears. Outside, the bullets stopped. There were no shouts between the attackers, no alarms, no barking of dogs or screaming of wounded. The sudden silence was total, broken only by the deep, shuddering breathing in the warm and muggy darkness.

A halogen beam flickered on, revealing the shocked faces of the team as David shone it around their retreat. A midsize room, crowded with desks and computer equipment. There were no windows.

"Did you *see* that?" Steve gasped, addressing no one in particular. "God, they wouldn't go *down,* did you see that?"

Nobody answered, and though they were out of immediate danger, Rebecca didn't feel her adrenaline slowing, didn't feel her heart settling back to anything approaching normal; it seemed that Umbrella had found a new application for the T-Virus. *And like it or not, we're going to have to deal with the consequences.*

They were trapped in Caliban Cove. And in this facility, the creatures had guns.

David took a final deep breath and exhaled it heavily, flashing the torch's light toward the door.

"I'd say we've been spotted," he said, hoping that he didn't sound as despairing as he felt. "Might as well see what we've gotten into. Rebecca, would you turn on the lights?"

She flipped the wall switch and the room snapped into blinding brilliance, overhead fluorescents pulsing to life. Blinking against the sudden glare, David surveyed the team, saw that Steve had one hand pressed to his chest.

"Are you hit?"

"Vest stopped it," he said, but he seemed more out of breath than the others, his face paler than it should have been.

Rebecca glanced at David with a questioning gaze. He nodded at her.

Doesn't appear that we have anywhere else to go. . . .

"Check him out. Anyone else?"

Nobody answered as Rebecca stepped up to Steve, motioning for him to take off the vest. David turned and looked around the room, measuring it against the memory of Trent's map and what little he'd seen from outside. There were a half dozen cheap metal desks, each with a computer and bits of clutter on top. The cement walls were undecorated and plain. There was another door on the west wall that had to lead deeper into the building.

"Karen, secure that," he said. They could check out the rest of the site once they'd decided what to do.

Once you've decided, Captain; perhaps you'd like to send them out for a swim? It can't be any worse than what you've already managed. . . .

David ignored the inner voice, perfectly aware of how badly he'd underestimated the situation. The team didn't need to see him wallow in self-doubt, it wouldn't help anything. The question was, what now?

"Let's talk," he said. "It doesn't look like we're facing an accident after all. What did the note say? The food was drugged, and something about a 'he' killing the others . . . is it possible that we're not looking at a T-Virus spill?"

Rebecca looked up from her examination of Steve's chest, the computer expert sitting on one of the desks in front of her. Steve winced as Rebecca's fingers circled the darkening bruise on his right pectoral. She smiled guiltily at him, shaking her head.

"You're okay. Nothing's broken."

She turned back to David, the smile falling away. "Yeah. If there'd been a release, that guy on the door, Ammon, would've been affected. But the Trisquads—if they're the result of experiments with the T-Virus, they'd have rotted away by now. It's been over three weeks since he wrote that note, we should be looking at piles of mush. Either it's a different virus—or someone's been taking care of them. Enzyme upkeep, maybe some kind of refrigeration. . . ."

David nodded slowly, following her reasoning. "And if that 'someone' had gone mad and killed everyone, why bother?"

"That corpse, waving at us," Karen said thoughtfully. "And the creature or creatures in the cove. It's like he expected people to come—"

"—but didn't mean for us to get very far," John finished.

The line from the note ran through David's mind, the words following the plea to stop "him."

'God knows what he means to do.' . . .

Steve had slipped his shirt back on, shivering from the damp cloth. "So what do we do now?"

David didn't answer him, not sure what to say. He felt so drained, so exhausted and uncertain. . . .

"I—our options are to get out or go deeper," he said softly. "Considering what's happened so far, I don't feel comfortable making that call. What do you want to do?"

David looked warily from face to face, expecting to see anger and disdain; he'd let them down, led them into a perilous situation without a contingency plan— all because he couldn't stand to see the S.T.A.R.S. tarnished. And now that they were trapped, he didn't know what to do.

The expressions they wore, as a group, were thoughtful and intent. He was surprised to see Karen actually smile, and when she spoke, her tone was brightly eager.

"Since you're asking, I want to figure this out. I want to know what happened here."

Rebecca was nodding. "Yeah, me, too. And I still want to get a look at the T-Virus."

"I wanna pick off a few more of those Tri-boys," John said, grinning. "Man, zombies with M-16s—night of the living death squad."

Steve sighed, pushing his wet bangs off his forehead. "Might as well keep looking; going back out isn't exactly safe. It's not the way I would've liked, but getting dirt on Umbrella *was* the original plan . . . yeah, I want to nail these bastards."

David smiled, feeling properly embarrassed at himself. He hadn't just underestimated the situation, he'd sorely underestimated his team.

"What do *you* want? Rebecca asked suddenly. "Really?"

The question surprised him anew—not because she'd asked, but because suddenly, he didn't have an answer. He thought about the S.T.A.R.S., about his obsession with his career and what it had already cost them. All he'd wanted for days was to feel as though his life's work had been meaningful, that it hadn't been wasted—and he'd convinced himself that uncovering the treachery within the job would lay his mind at rest, as if rooting out the corruption would somehow prove that he wasn't worthless.

I've worshipped at the altar of the organization for so

long . . . but isn't this the reason why, the real purpose? Here, in this room, on these faces?

He studied her curious, sharp gaze, felt the rest of them watching him, waiting.

"I want for us to survive," he said finally, truthfully. "I want for us to make it out of here."

"Amen to that," John muttered.

David remembered what he'd told the Raccoon team, about each of them doing what they did best if they meant to succeed against Umbrella. He'd said it to get Chris's approval of his operation, but it was a truth that applied to all of them.

Get to it, Captain. . . .

"John, you and Karen take a look around the building, check the doors, be back in ten. Steve, boot up one of those computers, see if you can find a detailed layout of the grounds. Rebecca, we'll go through the desks. We want maps, data on Trisquads, T-Virus, anything personal about the researchers that might tell us who's behind all this."

David nodded at them, realizing that he felt clearer and more balanced than he had in a long, long time.

"Let's do it," he said. To hell with the S.T.A.R.S. They were going to take Umbrella down.

Dr. Griffith might not have even noticed the security breach if it hadn't been for the Ma7s; it seemed that they were useful after all, though not in the way they'd been intended.

He'd spent most of the day in the lab, dreamily pondering the pressurized canisters standing by the entrance, the shining steel glittering seductively in the soft light. Once he'd made the decision to let the virus go, he'd realized that there was really nothing else he needed to do. The hours had flown by; each glance at the clock had been a surprise, though not an unpleasant one. He'd be the first, after all, the first convert to the new way of the world. With that in front of him, the only task with which he needed to concern himself was getting the canisters up to the lighthouse—and with the doctors waiting silently, patiently by, even that was taken care of. Just before dawn, he'd give them their final instructions—and then proudly lead the human species into the light, into the miracle of peace.

It had been the thought of the Ma7s that had finally drawn him out into the caves, the only concern he hadn't already dismissed as trivial. He'd already made a mistake with the Leviathans; once he'd taken over the facility, he'd lowered the cove gates on impulse, wanting them to be as free as he'd felt. It wasn't until the next day that he'd realized Umbrella might find out and come looking, effectively putting an end to his plans. He'd continued to send in weekly reports to keep up appearances, but there was no good explanation for the "escape" of the four creatures. It had been sheer luck that the Leviathans had returned on their own.

The Ma7s were a different matter entirely, of course. They were too violent, too unpredictable to be let out. But letting them starve to death in their cage didn't seem right, particularly not when they, too, would enjoy the effects of his gift; it wasn't their choice to exist as creatures of destruction, even to exist at all. And since he'd played a small role in their creation, he felt a responsibility to do *something* for them. . . .

He'd stood in front of the outer gate for quite some time, considering the problem as all five of the animals hurled themselves repeatedly at the heavy steel mesh, their strange, mournful howls echoing through the damp and winding caves. There was a manual lock release near the enclosure, another in the lab—but there was no way to loose them from the lighthouse, and he certainly couldn't let them out before he got to safety. He *could* send one of the doctors to do it, but the 7s had a much slower metabolism than a human's, and there was a risk that they would get to him before they made the change. A month before his takeover of the compound, Dr. Chin and two of her vet techs had made the mistake of trying to tend to one of the sick ones; it was a bad way to die, and although he'd be oblivious to the pain once he'd made the transition, he meant to stay with the new world for as long as possible.

Griffith had finally decided that euthanasia was the only reasonable choice. It was a reluctant decision, but he could see no alternative. Although the lab was well stocked, poisons weren't his forte, so he'd decided to look up the information on the mainframe—and there, in the cold comfort of the sealed laboratory, he'd discovered that his sanctuary had been invaded.

He sat in front of the computer in a kind of shock, staring at the blinking cursor that indicated system use in one of the bunkers. There was no chance that it was a mistake. Except for the lab terminals, the rest of the compound had been powered down weeks ago. Umbrella had come.

The first emotion to break through his stunned astonishment was rage, a sweeping, red-hot fury that tore away all reason, descending over him like a blinding fire. For a few moments, he was lost, his body taken over by the primal force, grasping and rending, tearing at the useless, meaningless things that fell beneath his burning fingers.

—they will NOT will NOT stop me will NOT—

When his hands touched the cool metal of the canisters, the fire turned to ash. The smooth, silver tanks were like a splash of reason, bringing him back to himself. His control returned as abruptly as it had gone, leaving him breathless and sweating.

My creation. My work.

Blinking, gasping, he found himself standing in a sea of ripped papers, broken glass, and torn circuitry. He'd managed to destroy the computer, the bearer of bad news, in pieces on the cold floor. On another day, he might have been ashamed at the hysterical tantrum, but on this, his eve of greatness, he allowed that the rage had been justified.

Justified, perhaps, but pointless. How will you keep them from stopping you? You can't release the strain here, and you can't risk taking it outside, not now . . . what are their plans? How much do they know?

He could find out easily enough. There were still two other terminals in the lab and he walked quickly to one of them, glancing at the mute doctors, sitting quietly by the airlock. If they'd even noticed his rampage, they gave no sign. He felt a small rush of hatred for them, for creating the useless Trisquads; the "unstoppable" guards had failed him now that he needed them most.

He sat down and turned on the monitor, impatiently waiting for the spinning umbrella of the company logo to disappear. The security network for the compound's system was based in the lab; he'd be able to see what the intruders were seeking without alerting them to his presence, if he could remember how to access the information. . . .

He tapped several keys, waited, then typed in his clearance number. After the briefest of pauses, lines of glowing green data spilled across the screen. He'd done it.

Seek, find, locate . . .

He frowned at the information, wondering why the hell anyone from Umbrella would be searching for the laboratory—and for that matter, why they'd try looking for that information in the mainframe at all. The system designers weren't idiots, there was nothing about the layout of the facility in the files. . . .

. . . and Umbrella would know it. Which means . . .

Relief coursed through him, cool and pure relief so great that he laughed out loud. He suddenly felt quite silly at his childish reaction to the breach. The searcher wasn't from Umbrella, and that changed everything. Even if they managed to find the lab—an unlikely proposition at best, considering its location—they wouldn't be able to gain entry without a key card. And Griffith had destroyed all of them—

—*except for Ammon's. His was never found.*

Griffith froze, then shook his head, a nervous smile on his face. No, he'd searched practically everywhere for the missing card, what were the chances that the interloper would stumble across it?

And what were the chances that they'd make it past the Trisquads, hmm? And what was Lyle up to during those hours when you couldn't find him? What if he did get a message out? You only checked for transmissions to Umbrella, but what if he contacted someone else?

Even as the dreadful, impossible thought occurred to him, the computer began to spit out information on the logic skills tests. The socio-psychological series tests that Ammon had designed.

Griffith felt his control slipping again. He clenched his hands into fists, refusing to give in; there was too much at stake, he couldn't afford to let his emotions take over, not now, he had to *think.*

I'm a scientist, not a soldier, I don't even know how to shoot, to fight! I'd be useless in combat, totally. . . . Unpredictable. Uncontrollable.

A slow grin spread across his features.

Blood was seeping from his fists, from where his ragged fingernails had dug into the heels of his hands, but he felt no pain. His gaze wandered around the open, silent laboratory, resting briefly on the airlock. Then to the blank, stupid faces of his doctors. To the cylinders of compressed air and virus, his miracle. And finally, to the controls for the mesh gate that led to the animal enclosure.

Dr. Griffith's smile widened. Blood pattered to the floor.

Let them come.

Πίπε

AS STEVE READ ALOUD, REBECCA SAW DAVID glance between his watch and the door several times. She didn't think it had been ten minutes, but it had to be close. John and Karen weren't back yet.

"'. . . where each is designed to measure application of logic, as combined index projective techniques with interval precision . . .'"

It was rather dry reading, apparently a facility report on the analysis of some kind of I.Q. test. It had obviously been written by a scientist—was, in fact, the kind of boring double talk that a lot of researchers tended to fall into when trying to explain anything more complicated than a chair. Still, it was what had come up when Steve had asked for information on "blue series." Since the room had yielded little else, Rebecca forced herself to pay attention, fighting off the nagging, quiet fear that had settled over her during the fruitless search.

Somebody had cleaned out the room, and done a very thorough job of it. She'd found books, staplers, pens and pencils, a ton of rubber bands and paper clips—but not a single piece of paper with writing on it, not a scrap of information to work with. Steve's computer search wasn't much better; no map and nothing at all on the T-Virus. Whoever had taken over the facility had apparently wiped out everything they might've been able to use.

Except for a shitload of dull psycho-babble, which so far hasn't even mentioned the word blue. How are we supposed to accomplish anything here?

Steve touched a key, then brightened considerably. "Here we go—

" 'The red series, when looked at on a standardized scale, is the most basic and simple, applicable up to an intelligence quotient of 80. The green series—' "

He broke off, frowning. "The screen just went blank."

Rebecca looked up from the mostly empty desk she'd been going through as David walked over to join Steve.

"System crash?" he asked worriedly.

Steve was still frowning, tapping at keys. "More like a program freeze. I don't think—hello, what's this?"

"Rebecca," David said quietly, motioning for her to come look.

She closed a drawer full of blank, unlabeled file

folders and moved over to stand behind Steve, bending down to read what was on the monitor.

The man who makes it doesn't need it. The man who buys it doesn't want it. The man who uses it doesn't know it.

"It's a riddle," David said. "Either of you know the answer?"

Before either of them could respond, Karen and John walked back into the room, both of them holstering their weapons. Karen held a sheet of torn paper in one hand.

"Locked up tight," John said. "Half a dozen offices, no windows at all and only one other external door, north end."

Karen nodded. "There were file cabinets in most of the rooms, but they were empty—except I found this in one of the drawers, stuck in a crack. It must have ripped off when the place was being cleaned out."

She handed the piece of paper to David. He scanned a few lines, his dark gaze taking on a sudden intensity.

He turned back to Karen. "This is all there was?"

Karen nodded. "Yeah. But it's enough, don't you think?"

David held up the torn sheet and started to read it out loud.

" 'The teams continue to work independently, but have shown a marked improvement since the modification of aural synapses.

" 'In Scenario Two, when more than one Trisquad is present, the second team (B) will no longer engage when the first (A) concludes (when target ceases to move or make sound).

" 'If the target continues to provide stimuli and A has discontinued the attack (lack of ammunition/disabling injury to all units), B will engage. If within range, additional patrols will be drawn to the attack and will engage in succession.

" 'At this time, we have not successfully managed to expand sensory ability to trigger desired behavior; the visual stimuli of Scenarios Four and Seven continue to be unproductive, although we'll be infecting a new group of units tomorrow and expect correlating results by the end of the week. It is our recommendation that we continue to further develop aural capabilities before considering heat-detection implantation—' "

"That's where it's torn off," David said, looking up.

Karen nodded. "It explains a lot, though. Why the team at the back door of the boathouse didn't do anything; the team out front was still firing. It wasn't until you and Steve took them out that the second group moved in."

Rebecca frowned, not liking the implications of the report for more than just the obvious; Umbrella's continued experimentation on humans. From what she'd seen in Raccoon, the T-Virus took seven or eight days to fully amplify in a host, the host then falling to pieces within a month—

So what's this about infecting a new group and getting data in a week? Or for that matter, implanta-

tion and sensory modification with the hosts they already have? There shouldn't be time for all that, the "units" should be disintegrating, way beyond learning new behavior. . . .

She bit her lip nervously, suddenly wondering what the researchers at Caliban Cove might have done with the virus. If they'd found a way to speed up the infective, perhaps tampered with the virion's fusion membrane, made it more cohesive . . .

. . . or somehow multiplied the inclusionary, allowing it to replicate exponentially . . . we could be looking at a strain that works in hours, not days.

It was a nasty thought, and one that she didn't want to consider until she had more information to go on. Besides, it wouldn't make a difference in their current situation; the Trisquads were just as deadly either way.

"The sign on the north door says we're in block C, whatever that means," John said, moving to the computer. "Did you find a map?"

Steve sighed. "No, but take a look. I asked for information on the blue series, and it started to give us a report on these I.Q. tests, coded by color—then this. I can't get anything else."

John peered at the screen, mumbling, ". . . man who makes it doesn't need it, buys it, doesn't want it, uses it, doesn't know it . . ."

Karen, who had been rereading the Trisquad material, looked up with sudden sharp interest. "Wait, I know that one. It's a casket."

Somehow, Rebecca wasn't surprised that Karen

knew the riddle; the woman struck her as someone who thrived on puzzles. They all gathered around as Steve quickly typed in "casket." The screen remained unchanged.

"Try 'coffin,'" Rebecca suggested.

Steve's fingers flew across the keys. As soon as he hit "enter," the riddle disappeared, replaced by:

BLUE SERIES ACTIVATED.

Then followed:

TESTS FOUR (BLOCK A), SEVEN (BLOCK D), AND NINE (BLOCK B)/ BLUE TO ACCESS DATA (BLOCK E).

"Blue to—Ammon's message," Karen said quickly. "That's it—the message received related to the blue series, then said, 'enter answer for key.' The answer was 'coffin'—"

"—and the test numbers are the key," David said. "There are three more lines in the message, then 'blue to access.' The lines must be the answers to the tests—the letters and numbers reverse, time rainbow, and don't count. Jill was right, it's all about something we're supposed to find."

Rebecca felt a rush of excitement as David grabbed a pen off the desk and turned over the scrap of the Trisquad report. The information they had finally made sense—Dr. Ammon's message actually *meant* something.

We can do this, we've got something solid now—

David drew five boxes in two lines, the same as on Trent's map, marking the southernmost box with the letter *C*. After a pause, he tentatively labeled the others, starting at the top left with *A* and going right to left, marking the test numbers next to each letter.

"Assuming that this is right side up," he said, "and that we need to complete the tests in order, we'll be moving in a stagger, a zig-zag between the buildings."

"And assuming the Trisquads don't have a problem with that," John said softly.

Rebecca felt her excitement dwindle, could see the same mixed emotions in the suddenly somber expressions they all wore, staring down at the boxes. She'd known that they were going to have to leave eventually, but had somehow managed to avoid thinking about it, putting it off until it was in front of them.

It was in front of them now. And the Trisquads would be waiting.

They stood at the north door in a dark and stuffy hallway, tightening bootlaces, adjusting belts, putting fresh clips into their Berettas. When David was ready, he turned to John and nodded.

"Give it back to me."

"You, Steve, and Rebecca will take the one on the left, northwest from here. Once we hear you get clear, Karen and I go straight across. If your guess is right, we'll be in block D; if you're upside down, block B. Either way, we secure the building, find the test number, and then wait for you to show up and give us the go-ahead."

"And if I don't . . ."

Karen took up the recital. "If we don't hear from you in half an hour, we come back here and wait for Steve and Rebecca. We complete the tests if it's feasible—"

John grinned, a white flash in the gloom. "—and then get our asses over the fence."

"Right," David said. "Good."

They were ready. There were infinite variables in the equation, any number of things that could go wrong with the simple plan, but that was always the case. There was no way to prepare for everything that *could* happen, not at this point, and the decision to split up was their best chance to avoid detection by the Trisquads. "Any questions before we go?"

Rebecca spoke up, her youthful voice tight with concern. "I'd like to remind everybody again to be extremely careful about what you touch, or what touches you. The Trisquads are carriers, so try to avoid getting close to them, particularly if they're wounded."

David shuddered internally, remembering what she'd told them before—that one drop of infected blood could hold millions, *hundreds* of millions of virus particles. Not a pleasant thought, considering. A nine-millimeter round could inflict a lot of damage. . . .

. . . *and they don't lie down when they're hit. The three by the boathouse just kept coming, walking and firing and bleeding* . . .

They were waiting for his signal. David shook the

thoughts off and thumbed the safety on his weapon, putting his other hand on the door latch.

"Ready? Quietly, now, on three—one . . . two . . . *three.*"

He pushed the door open and slipped outside into the cool night air and the whisper of ocean waves. It was much brighter than before, the almost-full moon having risen high, bathing the compound in silvery blue light. Nothing moved.

Straight in front of him about twenty meters away was John and Karen's destination, and he was relieved to see a door set into the concrete wall facing block C; they wouldn't have to go around to get inside.

David edged away from the door to his left, hugging the narrow shadow of the wall. He could just make out the front of the building he hoped was A, tall, wind-bent pines to the left and behind it. There was a darker shadow midway along its length, a door, and no cover in the thirty-plus meters that spanned the distance. Once they stepped away from C, they'd be totally vulnerable.

If there's a team between the two lines of buildings . . .

He shot a glance back, saw Rebecca and Steve tensed and waiting behind him. If they were going to walk into a corridor of fire, at least he'd be in front; Steve and Rebecca should have time to get back to cover.

He took a deep breath, held it—

—and broke away from the wall, running in a low crouch for the dark square of the block's entry. Shapes of pallid light and shadow blurred past. His entire being was waiting for the flash of an automatic, the *crack* of fire, the sharp and piercing pain that would take him down—but it was silent and still, the only sound the violent stammer of his heart, the rush of blood through his veins. Seconds stretched an eternity as the door loomed closer, larger—

Then the latch was under his fingers and he was pushing, bursting into a stifling blackness, spinning around to see Rebecca and then Steve come lunging in after him.

David closed the door quickly but quietly, sensing the emptiness of the dark room, the lack of life—and then the smell hit him. Either Steve or Rebecca gagged, a dry bark of involuntary revulsion as David snatched for the torch, already dreading what he knew they would see.

It was the same terrible stink that they'd come across in the boathouse but a hundred times more powerful. Even without the recent reference, David knew the odor. He'd experienced it in a jungle of South America and in a cultist's camp in Idaho, and once, in the basement of a serial killer's house. The smell of rotting, multiple death was unforgettable, a rancid bile like sour milk and flyblown meat.

How many, how many will there be?

The beam snapped on and as it found the tottering, reeking pile that took up one corner of the large storage room, David saw that there was no way to be certain; the bodies had started to melt into one another, the blackened, shriveling flesh of the stacked corpses blending and pooling from the humid heat. Maybe fifteen, maybe twenty. . . .

Retching, Steve stumbled away and threw up, a harsh and helpless sound in the otherwise quiet room. David quickly took in the rest of the chamber, finding a door against the back wall, the letter *A* blocked across it in black.

Without another look at the terrible mound, he hustled Rebecca toward the far door, grabbing Steve as they passed. Once they were through, the smell faded to barely tolerable.

They were in a windowless corridor, and though there was a light switch next to the door, David ignored it for the moment, catching his breath, letting the two young team members collect themselves.

Apparently, they'd found the Umbrella workers of Caliban Cove; all but at least one of them, anyway— and David decided that if they ran across *him*, he'd shoot first and not bother with any questions at all.

Karen and John stood at the door for a full minute after the others had gone, cracked open just wide enough for them to listen. Cool air filtered through the opening, the far away hiss of waves—but no shots, no screams.

Karen let the door close and looked at John, her pale features masked in the dim light. Her voice was low, even, and terribly serious. "They're in by now. You want to take lead, or would you prefer if I went first?"

John couldn't help himself. "My women always go first," he whispered. "Though I prefer it when we go together, if you know what I mean."

Karen sighed heavily, a sound of pure exasperation. John grinned, thinking about how easy she was. He knew he shouldn't devil her, but it was hard to resist. Karen Driver kicked ass with a weapon and she was sharp as a tack in the brains department, but she was also one of the most humorless people he'd ever known.

It's my duty to help her lighten up. If we're gonna die, might as well be laughing as crying. . . . A simple philosophy, but one he held dear; it had gotten him through many an unpleasant situation in the past.

"John, just answer the goddamn question—"

"I'll go," he said mildly. "Wait till I get through, then follow."

She nodded briskly, stepping back to let him by. He briefly considered telling her that he'd greet her at the door wearing nothing but a smile, but decided against it. They'd worked together for almost five years, and he knew from experience that he could only go so far before she got pissy. Besides, it was a good line, and he didn't want to waste it.

As soon as his hand closed over the latch, he took a deep breath, letting his sparkling wit take a back seat to what he thought of as his "soldier mind." There was humor, and then there was conquering the enemy—and while he enjoyed both immensely, he'd learned long ago to keep them separate.

Gonna be a ghost now, gonna slide through the dark like a shadow. . . .

He gently pushed the door open. No sound, no movement. Holding his Beretta loosely, he stepped away from the building and moved quickly through the silvery dark, fixing on the door that was scarcely twenty steps away. His soldier mind fed him the facts, the cool wind, the soft tread of boots against dirt, the smell and taste of the ocean—but his heart told him that he was a ghost, floating like an invisible shadow through the night.

He reached the door, touching the clammy metal bar with steady fingers—and it wouldn't move. The entrance was locked.

No panic, no worry, he was a shade that no one could see; he'd find another way in. John held up a hand, telling Karen to wait, and edged smoothly to his right.

Silent and easy, shadow without form . . .

He reached the corner and slid around, letting his heightened senses continue to feed him information. No movement in the whispering night, the rough feel of concrete against his left shoulder and hip, the steady pump of exhilaration and fluidity in his muscles. There was another door, facing the broad, glimmering openness of the sea, cool light matte against metal.

Rat-atat-atat—atat!

Bullets hit the dirt at his feet. John spun and leaped

backward, flattening himself against the wall as he grabbed for the latch. Walking from the direction of the boathouse, a line of three—

—and John tore the door open and jumped behind it, heard the clatter of .22 rounds smash into the metal, stopped inches from his body by the explosive *ping-ping-ping* that rattled the door.

He held the door open with his foot, took a split-second look around the edge and targeted the flash of light, squeezing the trigger as chips of concrete and dust flew from the wall. The nine-millimeter jumped, a part of his hand, and he was an animal now, at one with the thundering rounds, the pull of his breath, the awareness of himself both as a man and a bringer of death.

Another look and the line was closer now, the three dark figures taking shape. John got off another shot, ducked behind the open door—and when he looked again, there were only two standing.

Snap.

Behind him.

John whirled around and saw them, two of them, ten feet away at the northeast corner of the building. Both held automatic rifles.

But made no move to fire.

He felt panic then, a screaming, whining beast in his gut that threatened to devour him from the inside out—

—holy shit—

The fusillade of the M-16s was still approaching, but he could see only the creatures that stood there, watching him with blank and rubbery eyes, wobbling on unsteady legs. The one on the left had only half a face; from the nose down was a liquid, pulpy mass of tissue, chunks of dark wetness hanging from strings of elastic flesh. The one on the right looked intact at first, if deathly white and dirty . . . until he saw the exploded mass of its belly, the limp, dripping snake of intestine flopped out against his bloody shirt.

—won't engage until team A finishes—

John stepped backward into the warm dark of the building, using one distant arm to hold the door open against the pair that still fired. He leaned out and aimed as carefully as he could manage, squashing the panic as best he could. Neither of the creatures moved to defend themselves, only stood there, teetering on rotting legs, watching him.

Bam! Bam!

Two clean head shots, explosively loud over the continuing rattle of the M-16s. Before they'd even hit the ground, John heard another nine-millimeter thundering through the darkness, drowning the automatic fire.

Karen—

He shot another glance around the door—and saw the crumpling figures of the engaged team a hundred feet away, one of them still firing as it fell, its rattling rifle aimed uselessly at the sky. Karen crouched out from between the buildings, handgun still pointed at the spasming shooter, her back to John.

—teams won't engage—

"Don't shoot him! Over here, leave him!"

She turned, a lithe and graceful spin, sprinting to meet him. As soon as she was through, he pulled the door closed, the *crack* of the automatic muted to a dull popping sound.

John sagged against the door as Karen fumbled for the lock, his brain still screaming at him that he'd seen the impossible, that he'd just killed two dead men, that there was nowhere he could put that information that wouldn't drive him insane—

—can't be, didn't believe, didn't believe it before, didn't know and they were DEAD they were ROTTING and they were—

Karen's ragged whisper broke the warm dark, broke through the cycling chain of his spinning, dizzying thoughts.

"Hey, John—was it good for you?"

He blinked, the words registering slowly.

"Going first, I mean," she added. "Was it everything you hoped it would be?"

He felt a creeping amazement take the place of the whirling, terrible thoughts, the confusion ebbing, the waters of his mind becoming clear again.

"That's not funny," he said.

After a beat, they both started to laugh.

✝ЕП

THE FARTHER AWAY THEY GOT FROM THE front of the concrete block, the less noxious the air, for which Rebecca was deeply grateful. She'd been seconds away from vomiting herself, the smell was that bad—a greasy, oily stench that seemed almost tangible, an entity in itself.

As they moved quietly through the well-lit hall, she found herself thinking again about Nicolas Griffith, about the story of the Marburg victims—and although there was no proof that he was behind the mass slaughter of the Umbrella people, she couldn't shake the feeling that he was responsible.

The corridor led them past several open rooms, each as barren and sterile as the building they'd come from. They passed an exit at the far side of the block, and after another turn in the hall, finally came to a door marked again with the letter *A,* and below it, 1–4. There were three triangles beneath the numbers, each a different color—red, green, and blue.

David opened the door, revealing a much shorter hall, stark fluorescent light spilling into the stale darkness; there were two doors, one on either side. Steve found the lights and turned them on, and Rebecca saw that there were more of the colored triangles on the door to their right. The other was blank.

"I'll take the test," David said. "Steve, you and Rebecca check out the other room, we'll meet back here."

Rebecca nodded, saw Steve do the same. He looked a little pale, but seemed steady enough, though he dropped his gaze when he noticed her looking. She felt a pang of sympathy for him, realizing that he was probably embarrassed for losing his lunch.

They opened the unlabeled door and stepped into yet another windowless room, as stuffy and warm as the rest of the building. Rebecca turned on the lights and a rather large office lined with bookshelves flickered into view. A steel desk sat in one corner next to a filing cabinet, the empty drawers standing open.

Steve sighed. "Looks like another bust," he said. "You want the desk or shelves?"

Rebecca shrugged. "Shelves, I guess."

He grinned almost shyly. "Just as well. Maybe I can find some breath mints or something in one of the drawers."

Rebecca smiled, glad that he'd made the joke.

"Save me one. I swallowed it down back there, but it was a close call."

They locked gazes, still smiling—and Rebecca felt a tiny shiver of excitement run through her as the second stretched, lingering a few beats longer than a more casual exchange.

Steve looked away first, but his color had returned, his cheeks slightly pinker than before. He moved to the desk and Rebecca turned to face a row of books, feeling a little flushed herself. There was a definite attraction there, and it seemed to be mutual—

—*and it's only about the worst time and place to consider it,* her mind snapped. *Secure that shit, pronto.*

The books were about what she might've expected, considering what they knew about the Trisquads and Umbrella. Chemistry, biology, a whole set of leather-bound texts on behavior modification, several medical journals. As Steve rummaged through the desk behind her, she ran her hand along the row, pushing the books toward the back of the shelf as she glanced over the titles. Maybe there was something hidden behind one of them.

. . . *sociology, Pavlov, psych, psych, pathology*—

She stopped, frowning at a slender black volume tucked between two larger books. No title. She pulled it out and felt her heart speed up as she opened the small book, seeing the spidery handwriting on the lined pages.

She flipped to the front, saw "Tom Athens" written in neat letters on the inside cover.

One of the guys on the list, one of the researchers!

"Hey, I found a diary," she said. "It belongs to one of the people from Trent's list, Tom Athens."

Steve looked up from the desk, his dark eyes flashing. "No shit? Go to the back, what's the last date?"

Rebecca ruffled through the pages to the end, scanning as she went. "Says July 18—but it doesn't look like he kept it regular. The one before that is July 9 . . ."

"Just read the last entry," Steve said. "Maybe it'll tell us what was going on."

She walked to the desk and leaned against it, clearing her throat.

"'July 18, Saturday. It's been a long and ridiculous day, the end of a long and ridiculous week. I swear to God, I'm going to beat the crap out of Louis if he calls one more stupid meeting. Today it was whether or not we should add a new scenario into the Trisquad program, as if we need another one. All he really wanted was to get it on paper, and the rest of it was his usual bullshit—the importance of teamwork, the need to share information so we can all "stay on the right track." I mean, Jesus, it's like he can't live with the concept that a weekly might go out without his name on it. And he hasn't done dick since the Ma7 disaster, except to try and convince everyone that it was Chin's fault; so much for not speaking ill of the dead. Sanctimonious prick.

"'Alan and I talked over the implants yesterday, that's going well. He's going to write up the proposal this week, and we're NOT going to let Louis touch it. With any luck, we'll get a green light by the end of the month. Alan figures the White boys are going to want to run it past Birkin, though God only knows why; B. doesn't give a shit what we're doing out here, he's off being brilliant again. I have to admit, I'm looking forward to his next synthesis; maybe we can work out some of the bugs in the Trisquads.

" 'There was a minor scare in D on Wednesday, in 101. Somebody left the refrigerator open, and Kim swears that there are some chemicals missing, though I'm starting to think she miscounted again. Hard to believe she's in charge of the infection process, the woman's a ditz and she's sloppy as hell when it comes to maintaining the equipment. I'm surprised she hasn't managed to infect the entire compound. God knows there's enough in there to do it.

" 'I should probably get over to D myself, make sure everything's ready for tomorrow. Got a new batch shipping in, and Griffith actually asked to watch the process; first time he's come out of the lab in weeks, first time he's *ever* taken an interest in what the rest of us are doing. I know it's stupid, but I still want him to be impressed; he's as brilliant as Birkin, in his own creepy way. I think he even intimidates Louis, and Louis is generally too stupid to scare.

" 'More later.' "

The rest of the pages were blank. Rebecca looked up at Steve, not sure what to say, her mind working to glean the relevant bits of information from the rambling tirade. There was something in there that bothered her, something that she couldn't quite place.

Missing chemicals. Infection process. The brilliant, creepy Dr. Griffith. . . .

She no longer had any doubt that Griffith had killed the others, but that wasn't what sent her internal alarms jangling. It was—

"Block D," Steve said, a look of anxious fear playing across his face. "If we're in A, Karen and John are in D."

Where there's enough of the T-Virus to infect the entire compound. Where the infection process took place.

"We should tell David," Rebecca said, and Steve nodded, both of them moving quickly for the door, Rebecca hoping desperately that John and Karen wouldn't find room 101—and that if they did, they wouldn't touch anything that could hurt them.

The test room was big, three of the walls lined with open-ended cubicles. Once he'd turned on the lights, he saw that the tests were clearly numbered and color-coded, the symbols painted on the cement floor in front of each one.

All of the red series was on his left, closest to the door. He saw brightly colored blocks and simple shapes on the tables in each cubicle as he walked past, heading for the back of the room. The green series lined the wall opposite, though he ignored it entirely. The back wall was marked with blue triangles, the number four test in the far right corner.

As he neared the back of the room, he heard a faint hum of power coming from the blue test area. There was a small computer on the table in number two, a keyboard and headset in three. As promised, the series was activated—though what they were connected to, he couldn't imagine.

Can't imagine and don't care. Once we solve these

little puzzles, we'll find whatever's been hidden for us and get out, away from this cemetery. It can't happen soon enough.

David had seen all he wanted to see of Caliban Cove. The corpses in the front hall had been bad, but it was the thoughts that they'd inspired that troubled him, made him so suddenly eager to get his team out. The Trisquads were dangerous and deadly, the monster in the cove's waters had been horrible—but somewhere in the facility lurked a monster of a different kind entirely, one that had murdered his own people and then stacked them like kindling in a dark place. That kind of insanity chilled him far worse than the immoral greed of Umbrella, and he was afraid of what such a man might do to the handful of soldiers trying to stop him.

We'll find the "material," probably notes on Umbrella, perhaps on the virus itself—and then break for the fence, get well away from this madness. Let the Feds handle the rest. If they're smart, they'll blow up the entire compound and gather the information from the ashes. . . .

He stopped in front of the last cubicle, returning his attention to the task at hand. He wasn't sure what he was expecting to see, but the set up of test number four surprised him nonetheless. A table and chair, utilitarian gray metal. On the table was a pad of paper, a pencil, and an inexpensive chess set, all of the pieces in place. As he stepped into the cubicle, he saw that there was a metal plaque set into the surface of the table, a string of numbers etched into the steel.

David sat in the chair, peering down at the numbers.

9-22-3//14-26-9-16-8//7-19-22//8-11-12-7

He frowned, looking up at the chess set and then back at the numbers. There was nothing else to look at; that was it. He quickly sorted through the clues of Ammon's message, wondering which was supposed to be the answer. Was it, "the letters and numbers reverse," or "don't count"? Since there didn't seem to be anything relating to time or a rainbow, it had to be one of the two. . . .

If the lines are in the same order as the tests, this is the letter and number reversal. But what letters, there aren't any—

David smiled suddenly, shaking his head. The numbers on the plaque didn't go any higher than 26; it was a code, and a fairly simple one.

He picked up the pencil and quickly jotted down the letters of the alphabet, then numbered them backward; A was 26, B, 25, all the way back to Zed, 1. Glancing back and forth between the plaque and the paper, he wrote down the numbers and then started to decipher the message.

R . . . E . . . X . . . M . . .

The final letter was a *T,* and he stared down at the sentence, then at the chess board. It seemed that somebody had a sense of humor.

REX MARKS THE SPOT.

"Rex" was Latin for "king."

White always goes first, so . . .

He reached out and touched the white king. As soon as his finger contacted the piece, it swiveled in place, turning around to face the back of the board. At the same time, there was a soft, musical tone from overhead. He looked up and saw a tiny speaker set into the ceiling.

Nothing else happened, no flashing lights or secret passageways opening up behind the wall. Apparently, he'd passed.

How anti-climactic.

It seemed like an awfully complicated test for something as supposedly mindless as a Trisquad zombie— though perhaps the researchers had been making plans for something else, something intelligent. . . .

It was an unsettling thought, and not one he wanted to ponder. He stood up and turned toward the front of the room—

—just as the door burst open, Rebecca and Steve hurrying in, wearing matching expressions of fear.

"What is it?"

Rebecca held up a book, talking fast. "We found a journal. It says that the strain of the virus used to infect the Trisquads is in block D, in room 101. Maybe everything's fine, but if John and Karen touch anything that's been contaminated—"

He'd heard enough. "Let's go."

They turned and he strode past them, leading them back the way they'd come, his thoughts racing. They had passed an exit on the far side of the building, he could send Steve and Rebecca to the next block over while he went to D, just as originally planned—only much faster, and now carrying the horrible, heavy fear that two of his people might accidentally uncover the T-Virus.

It won't happen, they'll be careful, the chances of one of them getting a cut and then touching something dangerous in a room that's bound to be marked as some kind of a laboratory . . .

The reassuring facts did nothing to ease his mind. They hurried toward the exit, a deepening knot of dread settling into the pit of David's stomach.

They stood in the bright corridor at the center of D block, silently listening for a sound that would tell them David had come. From their position, they should be able to hear any one of the three external doors being used. After securing the building and finding the test room, she and John had chocked open all of the passages that led to the block's exits.

Karen checked her watch and then rubbed her eyes, feeling a bit worn out from all of the night's events, and still sickened by what they'd found in room 101. Even John seemed unusually subdued, and definitely quieter than normal. He hadn't cracked a single joke since they'd walked back to begin their wait.

Maybe he's thinking about the gurneys, fixed with bloody restraints. Or the syringes. Or the surgical equipment heaped in the sink. . . .

They'd found the test room first, a large chamber filled with little tables, each marked with numbers between five and eight; Karen had been somewhat disappointed to see that the blue series number seven was just a handful of colored tiles with letters on them, half of them upside down and unreadable. All the colors corresponded to a rainbow's, though there were two extra violet tiles in the heaped pile. Since they couldn't risk messing with it until David had completed the first test, she'd reluctantly turned away, suggesting that they check out the rest of the block.

They'd gone through a couple of offices, empty, and a cluttered coffee room, where they'd found a box of incredibly moldy donuts and little else. It had been the chemical lab that had told them the most about what kind of place Umbrella had created—and although Karen didn't believe in ghosts, the room had given her a feeling like nothing she'd ever experienced before; it was haunted, plain and simple, haunted by the misery of fear and the cold, nazi-esque precision of scientists committing atrocities against their fellow man—

"You thinking about that room?" John asked softly.

Karen nodded, but didn't say anything. John seemed to sense her unspoken desire not to talk about it, for which she was thankful. The weight of her good luck charm was the only other comfort she felt at the moment, and she longed to take it out, to feel reassured by memories of her father and successful missions gone by. Anything to take her mind off the lab room. . . .

The outer door to 101 was clearly marked with a biohazard symbol and they'd briefly discussed not going in at all, John arguing against entering a possibly contaminated environment. Karen had pointed out that neither of them had any cuts or abrasions, and that they might find something about the T-Virus to take with them. The truth was, she couldn't stand to let such an opportunity pass; she wanted to see what was behind the closed door, because it was there. Because leaving it unopened would get under her skin.

John had finally agreed and they'd gone in, stepping into a small entryway that was draped with sheets of heavy plastic. There were shower nozzles overhead and a drain set into the floor; a decon area. A smaller second door had opened up into the room itself, leading them into a mad scientist's dream.

Glass, crunching underfoot. A tired smell of anxious sweat beneath the acrid odor of bleach. . . .

John found the lights and even before the large room snapped into view, Karen felt her heart start to pound. There was a dark tension that filled the air, a sense of foreboding that radiated from the very walls. It looked like a dozen other lab facilities she'd worked in; counters and shelves, a couple of metal sinks, a large, stainless steel refrigeration unit in one corner with a lock on the handle. And somehow, that was the worst—that the environment was so familiar, a place she'd always felt at home.

The few differences were dramatic ones. The room was dominated by a stainless autopsy table, fitted with velcro restraints—and there were two additional hospital gurneys next to it, likewise fitted. As she walked over to look at one of them, she saw the dark, dried stains at either end; the thin pad was soaked with blood from where a man's ankles and wrists would be.

In the back of the room was a cage the size of a large walk-in closet, heavy bars surrounding an unpadded bench. Next to the cage, several slender poles leaned against the wall, each a meter or so in length—and tipped with hypodermic needles. They were the kinds of instruments used to drug wild animals, allowing the person operating them not to get within reach.

Karen looked down at the gurney, lightly touching the long-dried stain, wondering what kind of person could have willingly participated in such an experiment. The crust of blood was old, powdery, and filled her with thoughts of what the victims must have endured, waiting in the cage, perhaps watching as some gloved madman injected a toxic, mutating virus into a helpless human being. . . .

It was a bad place, a place of evil deeds. They'd both felt it, both been affected by the realization of what had gone on there—

Karen's right eye itched, distracting her from the terrible remembrance, drawing her back to the present. She rubbed at it, then looked at her watch again. It had been only twenty minutes since the team had split, though it felt longer—

There was a sound of a door opening, followed by David's excited shout through the corridor. He'd come in through the west entrance.

"Karen, John!"

John grinned at her, and she felt a wave of relief; David was okay.

"Here! Keep walking!" John called back. "Take a right at the tee!"

His footsteps pounded through the hall. In a few seconds, he appeared at the corner and jogged toward them, his face tight with concern.

"Is everything—" Karen started to ask, but David cut her off.

"Did you find the laboratory room? Room 101?"

John frowned, his smile fading. "Yeah, it's back the way you came—"

"Did either of you touch anything? Do you have any cuts, any small wounds that might have come in contact with anything?"

Their confusion must have shown. David spoke quickly, looking back and forth between them. "We found a journal, naming it as the room where they were infecting the Trisquads."

John smiled again. "Well, no shit. We figured that much out in about two seconds."

Karen held out her hands, turning them over for David to see. "Not a scratch."

David exhaled sharply, his shoulders sagging. "Oh, thank God. I had the worst feeling all the way over that something had happened. We found the researchers in block A; Ammon was right, he killed them—and our 'he' has a name now. Rebecca seems certain that it's Nicolas Griffith. He was the one she recognized from Trent's list, and he has a rather sordid history, she can fill you in when we regroup. . . ." He shook his head, a wavering smile on his lips. "I just—I suppose I let my imagination run wild for a moment."

John smiled wider. "Jeez, David, I had no idea you cared. Or that you thought we'd be stupid enough to stick ourselves with dirty needles in a place like this."

David laughed, a soft, shaky sound. "Please accept my sincerest apologies."

"Where are Steve and Rebecca?" Karen asked.

"Probably in the next test area by now. I saw them safely off to block B before I came here . . . did you find test seven?"

"This way," John said, and as they started down the hall, he began to recount their run-in with the Trisquads.

Karen followed, rubbing at the maddening, elusive itch in her right eye. She must have irritated it with all of the rubbing, it seemed to be getting worse. And to top things off, she felt a headache coming on.

She wiped at her eye, sighing inwardly at the timing. She never got headaches unless she was coming down with something. The swim in the ocean must have set her up nicely for a cold—and from the building throb in her head, it was going to be a nasty one.

ELEVEN

AFTER HE'D INSTRUCTED ATHENS AND SENT him on his way, he'd prepared the syringes and decided on a place to hide. There was nothing left for him to do but wait. In spite of his earlier feelings of confidence, he was nervous now, pacing through the lab restlessly. What if Athens had forgotten how to load a rifle? What if the enclosure release didn't work, or the intruders had the firepower to stop the Ma7s? He'd tried to prepare for every possibility, each plan unfolding into a backup—but what if everything failed, if all of them fell through?

I'll kill them myself, I'll strangle them with my bare hands! They will not stop me from doing what must be done. They can't—not after all I've accomplished, not after everything I've been through to get to where I am. . . .

For the second time that day, he flashed back to the takeover of the compound . . . the strange, vivid images of that bright and sunny day less than a month ago. Instead of blocking the thoughts as he'd done before, he let them come, inviting them in—to remind him of what he was capable of doing when the need arose. He abruptly stopped pacing and moved to a chair, collapsing into it and closing his eyes.

A bright and sunny day . . .

Once he'd realized what had to be done, he'd planned it for over two weeks, working over each detail tirelessly until he'd been satisfied that every variable had been addressed. He'd spent time reading about the Trisquads and going through the master logs, memorizing the routine of the facility. He'd watched the habits of his colleagues, learned their schedules until he could have recited them backward. He'd stared for hours at the sketches he'd made of each building, walking through them in his mind a thousand times. After careful consideration, he chose a date—and several days before, he'd slipped into the Trisquad processing room and stolen several small vials of extremely powerful medication.

Kylosynthesine, Mamesidine, Tralphenide—animal tranquilizers and a synthesized narcotic, some of Umbrella's finest work. . . .

It had only taken him an afternoon to get the mix the way he'd wanted it, just as he'd hoped. Then he'd waited, much as he was waiting now. . . .

The day before his plan was to unfold, he'd watched a Trisquad processing and then asked Tom Athens to come to the lab after dinner to privately discuss some thoughts he'd had on intensifying the suggestibility factor. Athens had been only too happy to accept, had listened eagerly to Griffith's description of the strain he'd already created—couched in hypothetical terms, of course—and after a nice, hot cup of laced coffee, Athens had become the first to experience Griffith's miracle.

Griffith smiled, remembering those initial glorious moments, the very first—and truly the most important—test of the strain's effectiveness. He'd told Athens that the only voice he could hear was that of Nicolas Griffith, that all others would be meaningless babble—and the suggestion had taken as easy as that. In the early hours of that fateful morning, he'd played a tape of one of Athens's own lectures for the compliant doctor—and the doctor had heard nothing but gibberish.

If it had failed, Griffith would have aborted the takeover, no one the wiser. He'd had an unfortunate accident in mind if the strain hadn't worked the way it was supposed to; Athens's body would have been found the next day, washed up on the rocky beach. But the incredible success of his creation had proved beyond doubt that it was meant to be, that he really had no choice but to continue. . . .

. . . *and so, the kitchen. The drops of sedative in the coffee cups, on the pastries, injected oh so carefully into the fruit and dissolved into the milk, the juices . . .*

Of the nineteen men and women who lived and worked in Caliban Cove, only one regularly skipped breakfast and didn't drink coffee, Kim D'Santo, the ridiculous young woman who worked with the T-Virus; Griffith had sent Athens to slit her throat as she lay sleeping, before the sun came up—

—*and it was a bright and sunny day, cloudless and clear as they gobbled their breakfasts and swallowed their coffee, walking out into the cool morning air, collapsing to the ground, many of them not making it out of the cafeteria before they stumbled and fell, a few crying out that they'd been poisoned as the words failed them and the drugs sent them to sleep*—

Griffith frowned, trying to remember what had happened next. He'd selected Thurman, unable to resist the petty pleasure of showing the good doctor what he'd created. Then Alan Kinneson, although he hadn't given the gift to Alan until later, keeping him sedated . . .

He knew the facts: Thurman and Athens had disposed of the workers and piled them in block A. Lyle Ammon had managed to keep himself hidden for a time, but had been found by the Trisquads later that evening. Griffith had eaten a late supper and gone to bed, waking up early to move papers and software to the lab. These were facts, things that he knew—but for some reason, the reality had blurred and he couldn't actually remember what he had seen, what had transpired for him the rest of that day.

Griffith searched through his thoughts, concentrating, but could only find the same hazy and uncertain images: a blinding mid-day sun, bathing the sleeping bodies in red. The scream of a gull over the cove, relentless and wild, calling to the hot wind. A coppery smell of dirt and, and—

—blood on my hands, on the scalpel that glittered wet and sharp and plunged into soft, yielding flesh of faces and bellies and eyes and later, the thundering crash of waves in the dark and the spool of fishing line and Ammon, Ammon, waving—

His eyes snapped open and the nightmare was over. Shaken, Griffith looked around at the cool, soft light of the laboratory. He must have dozed off for a moment, must have. Yes, that was it. He'd fallen asleep and had a terrible dream.

He looked at the clock, saw that only a few moments had passed since he'd sent the two doctors out. He felt a rush of relief, realizing that he hadn't been asleep for very long—but as the relief ebbed, he felt the nervousness slip back into his body, jittering and pulsing anxiety about the intruders that had come to his facility.

They won't stop me. It's mine.

Griffith stood up and started to pace restlessly, back and forth, waiting.

The "time rainbow" test, number seven, took only a moment longer to complete than test number four, what David had started to think of as the "chess test." John and Karen had shown him to the small table in the big room, standing behind him as he'd uprighted the colored tiles and laid them out. Beneath the heap of nine rainbow-shaded pieces was an elongated indentation, perhaps a foot long and two inches across; it was clear that just seven of the tiles would fit.

Seven colors in the rainbow, seven tiles. Simple. So why are there nine of them?

David ordered the pieces by their colors, placing them in a row beneath the indentation. Each bore a different letter on the top, inked in black. Red, orange, yellow, green, blue, indigo—

—and three violet tiles with three different letters.

"Is it supposed to spell something?" John asked.

Going from left to right, the first six tiles read, J F M A M J.

"Not in English," Karen said mildly.

The three violet pieces were J, M and F.

David sighed. "It's one of those where you have to figure out the next in the series," he said. "Apparently relating to time. Any thoughts?"

John and Karen both stared down at the puzzle, studying the letters; he wondered if they were as tired as he was starting to feel. John seemed distinctly less chipper than usual, and Karen looked fairly wiped out, her skin pale and gaze somewhat distant.

Of course they're tired, but at least they're making an attempt . . .

David looked back at the colored pieces and tried to focus, but couldn't seem to manage a single coherent idea. It had been an awfully long day, periods of intense concentration interspersed with violent rushes of adrenaline. He'd run through fear, self-doubt, determination and then fear again, plus a handful of less clear-cut emotions. Now he just felt frazzled, waiting to see what would come next. . . .

John grinned suddenly, a triumphant light in his eyes. "The letters stand for the months—January, February, March, April, May, June—July. It's J, the last letter is J."

"Brilliant," David said. He started to place the tiles in the indentation as John nudged Karen with his elbow, still grinning. "And you thought all I was good for was easy sex."

As usual, Karen didn't bother answering. Relieved to be through the second test, David pushed the last piece into place. There was a faint *click* and the rainbow lowered very slightly, perhaps a millimeter. From above them, a gentle chime sounded from a speaker, this one hidden by a fluorescent bar.

"That all I get?" John quipped. "No parade?"

David stood up, smiling tiredly. "I felt the same way with the other one. We should get moving, see how Steve and Rebecca are making out—"

"Interesting way of putting it, David," John said, chuckling. "Nice one."

It took David a moment to get it, though Karen rolled her eyes almost immediately—then scratched at them. When she took her hand away, David saw that her right eye was extremely bloodshot. The left was also slightly discolored, though not as badly.

She noticed his scrutiny and smiled at him, shrugging. "I irritated it somehow. It itches, but it's fine."

"Don't rub it, you'll make it worse," David said, leading them toward the door. "And have Rebecca take a look when we get across."

They walked back into a connecting corridor and started for the back exit, David steeling himself for another dash across the compound. By his count, they'd managed to take down three of the Trisquads in full; three men outside of the boathouse and a fourth on the run to the first building, then John and Karen's five between blocks C and D.

Useful information, if you happen to know how many of the squads there were to begin with.

He ignored the inner sarcasm as they reached the metal door, Karen leaning back to turn off the overhead light. They pulled out weapons and took deep breaths, preparing—and David felt a familiar sensation wash over him, one that he'd experienced before in tight situations but had never been able to name. It wasn't a feeling so much as a state of existence—and although not a religious man, it was the closest thing he'd found to a belief in fate, a sense that there were patterns at play beyond the realm of human influence.

Whatever was going to happen, whatever was already happening even as they readied themselves to step back outside—all of the deciding factors were now firmly in place, interlocking like pieces of a puzzle. He felt it with a certainty that denied reason. It was as though a great wheel of chance that determined outcome, that would show them life or death, success or failure, had been set into motion and was now spinning toward its inevitable conclusion—only instead of slowing down, the wheel would turn steadily faster, speeding up as it revealed to them what the cosmos had planned.

In the past, he'd often found comfort in the sudden awareness of that spinning wheel, the undefinable sense that the outcome had been decided and all anyone could do was watch it unfold. When he'd been a child and his father had been on one of his drunken, abusive rampages, the belief in a bigger picture had sometimes been the only thing that saved him from total despair. This time, though . . . this time, it felt like a terrible thing, a dark and whirling carnival ride that they had boarded by mistake, not realizing the truth until it was too late—that they couldn't go back, and there was no avoiding whatever lay ahead.

We hang on, then. We do what we can.

David stepped to the door, flicking the Beretta's safety off. Whether or not they had any control over what was to come, Rebecca and Steve were waiting.

The test room was quiet except for the soft hum from the machines marked with blue numbers, nine through twelve, and the occasional rustle of a turning page as Rebecca went through Athens's journal. Steve sat on the edge of a table and watched her read, his thoughts restless and uneasy as they waited for the others to show up. His chest ached mildly, both from the small caliber round he'd taken earlier and the anxious build of worry for John and Karen.

After a quick look at the other rooms in the building, they'd both agreed that the test room was the place to wait. It seemed that block B of the Umbrella facility was mostly devoted to surgical aspects of the bio-weapons research, the rooms all white and steel, ominously stark and unpleasant. Although the building was as stuffy and warm as the others they'd been in, Steve had felt a physical chill as they'd passed the empty operating rooms—as if the chambers themselves had taken on the characteristics of the T-Virus creatures. Cold and lifeless and somehow mindlessly black with purpose. . . .

Rebecca looked up, her eyes flashing with excitement. "Listen to this:

" 'They're still waiting for our feedback on expansion ever since Griffith revved up the amp time. We've got the space for up to twenty units, but I'm going to hold strong on a max of twelve; we wouldn't be able to concentrate on training more than four squads at a time. Ammon said he'll back me up if there's any hassle.' "

Steve nodded, half dismayed and half relieved by the information. They'd already knocked one of the Trisquads out of the running, plus seriously wounded or killed a couple of the individuals on another team; that was good. On the other hand, it meant that there were still a couple of the squads roaming around out there—

—*unless they're currently "engaged" with David and the others. . . .*

He scowled inwardly, grasping for something else to think about.

"Do you know what that means, 'revved up the amp time'?"

Rebecca nodded slowly, worry creasing her brow. "I'm pretty sure he means that Griffith sped up the amplification process. Amplification is the term for a virus's spread through a host."

That didn't sound like something he wanted to think about either. By some unspoken agreement, they hadn't talked about the possibility of John or Karen being infected since David had left.

"Great. You find anything else in there?"

She shook her head. "Not really. He mentions the Ma7s a couple of times, but nothing more specific than that they're a T-Virus experiment that didn't work. And he's definitely kind of an asshole."

"Kind of?"

Rebecca smiled briefly. "Okay, that's an understatement. He's a money-hungry, amoral bastard."

Steve nodded, thinking about the partial report they'd found on the Trisquads—and for that matter, the very existence of the facility. Calling the T-Virus victims "units," setting up operating rooms and aptitude tests to run them through like rats in a maze—

—*it's like they can't acknowledge that they're performing their experiments on human beings, on real people. . . .*

"How could they do this?" he asked softly, as much to himself as to Rebecca. "How did they sleep at night?"

Rebecca gazed at him solemnly, as if she had an answer but wasn't sure how to say it. Finally, she sighed. "When you specialize in one field, particularly when it's a field that demands linear thinking and a very defined focus on only one tiny element of something—it's kind of hard to explain, but it's frighteningly easy to get lost in that single element, to forget there's a world outside of that element. When you spend your days looking into a microscope, surrounded by numbers and letters and processes . . . some people get lost. And if they were unstable to begin with, the ambition to pursue that element can take over, making everything else unimportant."

Steve saw what she was getting at and was impressed anew with how thoughtful she was, how clearly she communicated herself. . . .

. . . all that and a smile that lights up a room; if—when we get out of this, I'm moving to Raccoon City. Or I'll at least find out if she's seeing anyone. . . .

There was a sound from somewhere in the building, footsteps. Steve pushed himself off the table and walked quickly to the door.

He leaned out into the corridor and heard David's voice calling through the empty block.

"In the back!" Steve shouted, then waited, anxiously watching the corner in the hall for David to walk into view, John and Karen both healthy and smiling beside him. Rebecca moved to stand next to Steve, and he saw the same concern and hope written across her delicate features.

Instinctively, he groped for her hand, feeling a tingling jolt as their fingers touched, half expecting her to pull away—but she didn't, leaning against him instead as she held his hand gently, her skin soft and warm on his.

John's booming voice preceded him down the corridor, loud and full of bright good humor. "Get your clothes on, kids, you've got company!"

She dropped his hand quickly, but the look that she flashed him more than made up for it—a sweet and wistful expression that made his heart skip a beat—but there was a maturity there, too, a realization of the circumstances they were in, an acknowledgment of priorities.

No more until we're out of here.

He nodded slightly, and they turned to wait for the others.

TWELVE

REBECCA COULD STILL FEEL THE LINGER-
ing warmth of Steve's hand in hers as David, John,
and Karen walked around the corner, John grinning
broadly.

"Sorry to crash, but we figured you guys could use a
little chaperoning," he said. "Nothing like young love,
though, am I right?"

As the three stepped into the room, Rebecca struggled to quash the blush she felt creeping up on her,
suddenly feeling horribly unprofessional. All they'd
done was hold hands, and only for a second—but
they were in the middle of an operation, in hostile
territory where even a moment's lapse of concentration could get them killed.

John must have picked up on her embarrassment.
"Ah, don't mind me," he said, his grin fading. "I'm

just giving Steve-o a hard time, I didn't mean anything by it—"

David interrupted, shooting John a pointed glance. "I think we have more important things to discuss," he said evenly. "We need to update, and I have a few things I'd like to go over."

He nodded toward the journal she still held. "They found the room, but didn't touch anything. Did you find anything else useful?"

She nodded, relieved by the news and glad for the change of subject. "It looks like there are only four Trisquads, though the entry that mentioned it is six months old."

David looked relieved. "That's excellent. John and Karen had another encounter outside of D, managed to get five of them—that means there may only be one team left."

They pulled chairs away from the small tables that lined the walls, forming them in a loose semi-circle in the middle of the room. David stayed standing, addressing them solemnly.

"I'd like to do a quick recap, to make certain we're all on the same page before we go any further. In short, this facility was used for T-Virus experimentation and has been taken over by one of the researchers for reasons unknown. The other workers have been killed and the offices purged of incriminating evidence. Rebecca believes that the biochemist Nicolas Griffith is responsible, and the fact that the grounds are still being patrolled suggests that he's alive, somewhere in the compound—though I don't feel we should concern ourselves with trying to find him. We've already completed two of the tests given to us by Dr. Ammon, through Trent, and my hope is that the 'material' he has hidden for us will be the evidence we need to formally charge Umbrella with criminal activity."

He folded his arms and started to pace slowly as he talked, glancing between them. "Obviously there's already plenty of proof that illegalities have occurred here; we could leave now and turn the matter over to federal authorities. My concern is that we still don't have enough hard evidence on Umbrella's involvement—other than the computer system's software and the journal that Steve and Rebecca found, Umbrella's name isn't on anything, and both of those could be explained away. My feeling is that we should continue with the tests and find whatever Dr. Ammon meant for us to have before we evac—but I want to hear from each of you about it first. This isn't an authorized op, we're not following orders here, and if you think we should go, we go."

Rebecca was surprised, could see that the others felt the same by their expressions. David had seemed so certain before, so enthusiastic about their chances. The look on his face now told a different story. He seemed almost apologetic about wanting to continue, and looked as though he wanted for one of them to suggest otherwise.

Why the change? What happened?

John spoke first, glancing at the rest of them before looking at David. "Well, we've made it this far. And if there's only one more group of zombies out there, I say we finish up."

Rebecca nodded. "Yeah, and we still haven't found the main lab, we don't know *why* Griffith did this—whether he suffered a psychotic break or is actually hiding something. We may not find out, but it's worth a look. Plus, what if he destroys more evidence after we've gone?"

"I agree," Steve said. "If the S.T.A.R.S. are as deeply involved with Umbrella as it looks, we're not going to get another chance. This may be our only opportunity to dig up a connection. And we're already so close, the third test is right here—we do that one, we're one step away from finishing."

"I'm up for it," Karen said softly.

At the strained sound of her voice, Rebecca turned to look at her, noticing for the first time that Karen didn't look so good. Her eyes were bloodshot, her complexion almost a pallor.

"Are you okay?" Rebecca asked.

Karen nodded, sighing. "Yeah. Headache."

Must be a migraine, she looks like hell. . . .

"What is it, David?" John asked abruptly. "What's eatin' you? You know something you're not telling us?"

David stared at them for a moment, then shook his head. "No, nothing like that. I just—I have a bad feeling. Or rather, a feeling that something bad is going to happen."

"Little late, don'tcha think?" John said, grinning. "Where were you when we got into the raft?"

David half-smiled in response, rubbing the back of his neck. "Thank you, John, I'd almost forgotten. So, it's decided then. Let's solve our next puzzle, shall we? Oh, Rebecca, take a look at Karen's eye while we're at it, it's giving her some trouble."

They stood up and moved toward the back of the room, for the table in the northwest corner marked with a blue nine. Steve and Rebecca had already looked when they'd found the room, though there was no clue as to what the test was—a small, blank monitor screen with a ten-key hooked to it sat on the metal table, an enigma.

Rebecca motioned for Karen to sit on the chair in front of test ten, the purpose of which also escaped her—it consisted of a circuit board wired to a plank and what looked like a pair of tweezers connected to it by a black wire. She bent down to take a look, frowning. The woman's right eye was extremely irritated, the pale blue cornea floating in a sea of red. Her eyelid had a bruised, swollen look.

She turned to ask for David's flashlight—and saw that as he sat down in front of the scheduled test, the screen flickered on, several lines of type appearing in the center of the monitor.

"Some kind of motion sensor—" Steve started to say, but David held up his hand suddenly, reading aloud what had appeared on the screen in a rapid, anxious voice.

"'As I was going to Saint Ives, I met a man with seven wives—the seven wives had seven sacks, the seven sacks held seven cats—the seven cats had seven kits; kits, cats, sacks, wives, how many were going to Saint Ives?'"

There was a digital readout on the screen, showing 00:49 and counting down. In the time it had taken David to read the question, eleven seconds had already ticked off the clock.

David stared at the screen, his thoughts racing furiously as the team leaned in behind him. Tension radiated from them, and David felt a sudden prickle of sweat break out across his forehead.

Don't count, that was the clue. But what does it mean?

"Twenty-eight," John said quickly. "No, wait, twenty-nine, including the man—"

Steve cut him off, talking just as fast. "But if they had seven kittens *each*, that would be forty-nine plus twenty-one, seventy, seventy-one with the man."

"But the message said don't count," Karen said. "If you're not supposed to count—does that mean don't add, or—wait, there's the man with the wives *and* the speaker, that's another one—"

Thirty-two seconds had elapsed. David's hand hovered over the key pad.

Think! Don't count, don't count, don't—

"One," Rebecca said quickly. "'As *I* was going to Saint Ives'—it doesn't say where the man with the wives was going. That's what it means, the clue—don't count anyone except the *one* who was going to Saint Ives!"

Yes, it makes sense, a trick question—
They had twenty seconds left.

"Anyone disagree?" David asked sharply.

No answer. David hit the key, entered it—

—and the countdown stopped, sixteen seconds to spare. The screen turned itself off. From somewhere overhead, the now familiar chime sounded.

David exhaled, leaning back in the chair. *Thank you, Rebecca!*

He turned around to tell her as much, but she was already bending to examine Karen's eye, fixated on her patient.

"I need a flashlight," she said, barely glancing around as John handed his to her. She turned it on, shining it into Karen's eye as the rest of them looked on silently, watching them. Karen didn't look well; there were dark circles under her eyes, and her skin had gone from pale to almost sickly.

"It's pretty inflamed . . . look up. Down. Left and right? Does it feel like there's something rubbing it, or is it more like a burn?"

"Actually, more like an itch," Karen said. "Like a mosquito bite times ten. I've been scratching it, though, that might be why it's so red."

Rebecca turned off the torch, frowning. "I don't see anything. The other one looks irritated, too . . . did it just start itching all of a sudden, or did you touch it, first?"

Karen shook her head. "I don't remember. It just started itching, I guess."

A look of sharp, almost violent intensity flashed

across Rebecca's face. "Before or after you were in room 101?"

David felt a cold hand clutch at his heart.

Karen suddenly looked worried. "After."

"Did you touch anything while you were in there, anything at all?"

"I don't—"

Karen's red eyes widened in sudden horror, and when she spoke, it was a breathless, quivering whisper. "The gurney. There was a bloodstain on the gurney and I was thinking about—I touched it. Oh, Jesus, I didn't even think about it, it was dry and I, my hand wasn't cut and oh my *God,* I got a headache right after my eye started itching—"

Rebecca put her hands on Karen's shoulders, squeezing them tightly. "Karen, take a deep breath. Deep breath, okay? It may be that your eye just itches and you have a headache, so don't jump to conclusions here, we don't know anything for sure."

Her voice was low and soothing, her manner direct. Karen blew out a shaky breath and nodded.

"If her hand wasn't cut . . ." John started nervously.

Karen answered him, her pale features composed but her voice trembling slightly. "Viruses can get into the body through mucous membranes. Nose, ears . . . eyes. I knew that. I knew that but I didn't think about it, I—wasn't thinking about it."

She looked up at Rebecca, and David could see that she was struggling to maintain her composure. "If I *am* infected, how long? How long before I become . . . incapacitated?"

Rebecca shook her head. "I don't know," she said softly.

David felt as though a raging blackness had enveloped him, a cloud of fear and worry and guilt so vast that it threatened to overwhelm his ability to move, even to think.

My fault. My responsibility.

"There's a vaccine, right?" John asked, his dark gaze darting between Karen and Rebecca. "There's a cure, wouldn't they have a shot or something here if someone got it by accident? They'd have to, wouldn't they?"

David felt a sudden surge of desperate hope. "Is it possible?" he asked Rebecca quickly.

The young biochemist nodded, slowly at first but then eagerly. "Yeah, it's possible. It's *probable,* they created it—"

She looked at David seriously, urgently. "We have to find the main lab, where they synthesized the virus, and quickly. If they developed a cure, that's where the information would be. . . ."

Rebecca trailed off, and David could see what she'd left unspoken in her troubled gaze; if there *was* a cure. If Dr. Griffith hadn't taken the information there, too. If they could find it in time.

"Ammon's message," Steve said. "In that note, he said we should destroy the lab—maybe he left us a map, or directions."

David stood up, his hope building. "Karen, are you feeling well enough to—"

"—Yes," she said, cutting him off, standing up. "Yes, let's go."

Her red eyes were bright with fervent intensity, a mix of despair and wild hope that made David's heart ache to see.

God, Karen, I'm so, so sorry!

"Double time," he said, already turning for the door. "Let's *move.*"

They quickly jogged for the front of the building, John's jaw clenched, his thoughts a grimly determined loop of angry intention.

No way some goddamn bug is taking Karen down, no chance, and if I find the bastard who set this nightmare up he's Dead, capital D, Dead meat. Not Karen, no way in hell. . . .

They reached the front door and silently drew weapons, checking them, tensely impatient for David to give the signal. Karen, always so cool and collected in times of stress, had a shocked vagueness about her, like she'd just been kicked in the gut and hadn't yet managed to take a breath. It was the same look that John had seen time and again on the faces of disaster survivors—the haunted disbelief in the eyes, the slack and terrible blankness of expression that spoke of a yawning emptiness deep inside. It hurt him to see her like that, hurt him and made him even angrier. Karen Driver wasn't supposed to look like that.

"I lead, John in back, straight line," David said softly.

John saw that he looked almost as freaked as Karen, though in a different way. It was guilt gnawing at their captain, he could see it in his reluctant gaze, the tight set of his mouth. John wished he could tell him that blaming himself was wrong, but there wasn't time and he didn't have the right words for it. David would have to take care of himself, just as they all would.

"Ready? *Go.*"

David pushed the door open and then they were slipping through, back into the gentle hiss of waves and the pale blue light of the moon. David, then Karen, Steve, Rebecca, and finally John, crouched and running across the packed dirt of the open compound.

There was darkness and the scent of pine, of salt, but John's soldier mind wasn't telling him anything he didn't already know as they pounded through the shadows. There was only anger, and fear for Karen—making the sudden blast of M-16 fire a total surprise.

Shit!

John dove for the ground as the thundering rattle opened up to their right, saw that they were just over halfway to block E as he rolled and started to fire. Then the air was filled with the blast of nine-millimeter rounds, crashing over the steady pulse of automatic rifles.

Can't see, can't target—

He found the muzzle flashes at three o'clock and jerked the Beretta around, squeezing the trigger six, seven, eight times. The stutter of orange-white light blocked the shooters from view but he saw one of the flashes disappear, heard the clatter decrease—

—and a rage overtook him, not the "soldier mind" but a blinding, screaming fury at the diseased attackers that far exceeded any he'd ever known. They wanted Karen to die, those numb, brainless nightmares wanted to stop them from saving her.

Not Karen. NOT KAREN.

A strange, feral howl beat at his ears as he pushed away from the dusty earth and then he was standing, running, firing. Only when he heard the shouts of the others, the Berettas except for his holding fire, did he realize that the howl was coming from him.

John ran forward, screaming as he fired again and again at the things that meant to slow them up, to kill them, to claim Karen as one of their own. His thoughts were no longer words, just an endless, formless negative—a denial of their existence and what had created them.

He charged ahead, not seeing that they had stopped firing, that they were falling, that the shadows had fallen silent except for the thunder of his semi and the scream that poured from his shaking body. Then he was standing over them and the Beretta had stopped crashing and jumping, even though he still pulled the trigger.

Three of them, white where there was no red, decayed flesh bursts covering their pitiful, wasted forms.

Click. Click. Click.

One of them had a face that was a mass of puckered scar tissue, twisting white risers of gnarled skin except for where a fresh, bloody hole had punched through its forehead. Another, one eye spattered against its withered cheek, pooling viscous fluid in the rotting cup of its ear.

Click. Click.

The third was still alive. Half of its throat was gone, tattered to pulp, and its mouth opened and closed soundlessly, opened and closed, its filmed dark eyes blinking slowly up at him.

Click.

He was dry-firing, the scream dying away in his ragged throat. It was the sound of the hammer falling uselessly against hot metal that finally released him from the rage—that, and the slow, helpless blink of the wretched thing at his feet.

It didn't know what it was. It didn't know who they were. Once it had been a man, and now it was rotting garbage with a gun and a mission it couldn't possibly understand.

They took his soul. . . .

"John?"

A warm hand on his back, Karen's voice low and easy next to him. Steve and David stepped into view, staring down at the gaping, blinking shell of humanity in the shaded moonlight, the last remnant of an experiment in madness.

"Yeah," he whispered. "Yeah, I'm here."

David trained his Beretta on the monster's skull and spoke softly. "Stand back."

John turned away, started walking back for their last destination with Karen at his side, Rebecca's slight form in front of him. The shot was incredibly loud, a booming *crack* that seemed to shake the ground beneath their feet.

Not Karen, oh please not one of us. That's no way to go out, no way to die—

Then David and Steve were with them and without speaking, they broke into a jog for block E, moving quickly through the emptiness that had claimed the night. The Trisquads were no more—but the disease that made them might even now be coursing through Karen's body, turning her into a creature with no mind, no soul, doomed to a fate worse than death.

John picked up speed, silently swearing to himself that if they found this Dr. Griffith, he was going to be awfully goddamned sorry that they did.

THIRTEEN

THE E BLOCK WAS NO DIFFERENT THAN THE first four they'd encountered, as bland and industrial and stale as the rest of them, a study in concrete efficiency. They moved quickly through the stuffy halls, turning on lights as they went, searching for the room that held the final clue to Dr. Ammon's secret. It didn't take long; almost half of the structure was taken up by an indoor shooting range, where David had found boxes of loaded M-16 mags—but no rifles to go with them. John had asked if he should retrieve the Trisquad's weapons, which Rebecca promptly vetoed. The rifles were hot, probably crawling with virus.

Like Karen's blood by now, streams of replicating virions bursting from cells, searching for new cells to attach to and use and destroy. . . .

"Here!" Steve called from farther down the winding corridor, and Rebecca hurried toward him, Karen and John not far behind. David was already standing with Steve by the closed door, the red, green, and blue triangles a sign that they'd hit on the right room. Steve's gaze seemed to seek her out, but was blank of all emotion except worry. She didn't mind, noted it only absently. Karen's infection, John's insane run at the Trisquad—there wasn't room in her for anything but the need to find the lab, to find help for Karen.

Steve opened the door and they filed inside, Rebecca continuing to watch Karen closely for signs that the virus had progressed—and wondering what she should do with the information she'd picked up so far about the amplification time. She didn't really have any doubts that Karen had been exposed, and knew that no one else did, either—but what should she say?

Do I tell her that it might only take hours? Do I pull David aside? If there's a cure, she has to get it before the damage is too great, before it starts to fry her brain—before it dumps so much dopamine into her that she stops being Karen Driver and becomes . . . something else.

Rebecca didn't know how to handle it. They were already doing all that they could, as fast as they could, and she didn't know enough about the T-Virus to assume anything. She also didn't want to see Karen any more terrified than she was already. The woman was doing her best to control it, but it was obvious that she was on the edge of a breakdown, from the desperation in her bloodred eyes to the growing tremor of her hands. And the Trisquads had almost certainly been injected with much larger amounts than Karen had been exposed to; maybe she had days. . . .

. . . *first symptoms in less than an hour? Don't kid yourself. You have to tell her, to warn her and everyone else of what could happen. Soon.*

She pushed the thought aside almost frantically, looking around at the room they'd entered. It was smaller than the test chambers they'd come across, and emptier. There was a long meeting table pushed to the back, a half dozen chairs behind it. In the front of the room was a small shelf coming off the wall, only a few feet long and a foot deep. There were three large buttons on the flat surface, red, green, and blue. The wall behind the shelf was tiled in large, smooth gray tiles made from some kind of industrial plastic.

"That's it," Steve said. "Blue to access."

With barely a second's hesitation, David walked to the counter and pushed the blue button—

—and a woman's voice spoke coolly from a hidden speaker above, startling them. It was a recording, the bland tone eerily reminding Rebecca of the final moments at the Spencer estate, the triggering system tape.

"Blue series completed. Access reward."

One of the tiles behind the shelf slid away, revealing a dark recess set into the concrete. As David reached into the hidden space, Rebecca felt a surge of frustrated anger and disgust for Umbrella, for what she realized they had done. It was despicable.

All those tests, all that work—set up to dole out treats to T-Virus victims. Get through the red series, good dog, here's your bone . . . and what was their reward, for making it through the tests? A piece of meat? Drugs, to ease their hunger? Maybe a brand new weapon for them to train with? Jesus, did they even understand what they'd been doing?

She saw the same curled sneers of horror and disgust on the faces of the others—and saw the same growing dismay as they watched David pull a single tiny item from the recess, what looked like a credit card with a slip of paper stuck to one side.

They gathered around him as he held the item up, his dark gaze heavy with an almost manic disappointment. It was a light green key card, the kind used to open electronic doors, blank except for a magnetic strip—and the scrawled words on the small square of paper said only:

LIGHTHOUSE-ACCESS 135-SOUTHWEST/EAST.

"Handwriting's the same as on Ammon's note," Steve said hopefully. "Maybe the lab is in the lighthouse. . . ."

"One way to find out," John said. "Let's go."

He seemed angry, the same look he wore since their discovery of Karen's exposure to the virus. After watching him charge the Trisquad outside, Rebecca almost hoped that they'd come across Dr. Griffith; John would tear him apart.

David nodded, slipping the card into his vest. The fear and guilt that he felt were obvious, playing across his features in a constant, twitching mask. "Right. Karen . . . ?"

She nodded, and Rebecca saw that her already pale skin had taken on a waxy tone, as if the top layers were becoming translucent. Even as she watched, Karen started to scratch absently at her arms. "Yeah, I'm good," she said quietly.

She has to know. She deserves to know.

Rebecca knew it couldn't wait any longer. Choosing her words carefully, aware of their limited time, she turned to Karen and spoke as calmly as she could.

"Look, I don't know what they've done with the T-Virus here, but there's a chance that you could start to experience more advanced symptoms in a relatively short amount of time. It's important that you tell me, tell all of us how you're doing, physically and psychologically. Any changes at all, we need to know, okay?"

Karen smiled weakly, still scratching at her arms. "I'm scared shitless, how's that? And I'm starting to itch all over. . . ."

She turned her red eyes to David, then to Steve and John before looking back at Rebecca. "If—if I start to act . . . irrationally, you'll do something, won't you? You won't let me—hurt anyone?"

A single tear slid down one pale cheek, but she didn't look away, her wet, crimson gaze as firm and strong as it had ever been.

Rebecca swallowed, struggling to sound confident and reassuring, awed by the bravery she saw in Karen's eyes—and wondering how much longer that bravery would hold up beneath the roar of the T-Virus running through her veins.

"We're going to find the cure before it comes to that," she said, and hoped that she wasn't telling Karen a lie.

"Move out," David said tightly.

They moved out.

The grounds of the facility were on a definite gentle slant, rising to the north, but as they left the E block and started for the towering black structure that perched over the cove, the curving slope became much steeper. The rocky soil angled up sharply, maybe as much as a thirty-degree incline, making the half klick walk into a hike. David ignored the strain in his back and legs; he was too worried about Karen and too busy tearing away at his own incompetence to bother with physical discomfort.

They were closer to the shimmering waters of the cove than they had been since climbing out of them, and the cool, whispering breeze off the moonlit surface would have been pleasant on some other night, in some other place. The swaying ripples of soft light and the soothing murmur of waves were almost a mockery of their desperate situation, such a sharp contrast to the chaos inside of him that he found himself almost wishing that there were still Trisquads roaming around.

At least then this would feel like the nightmare it is. And I could do something, I could fight back, defend them against something tangible. . . .

Ahead of them, the rising land curled around to the east, dropping away to a foaming sea far below. The cove itself was fairly calm, but the sound of waves smashing against the cliffs grew louder as they hurried on, approaching where the ocean met towering, cave-riddled rock walls. John had taken the lead, Karen next and then the two younger team members. David brought up the rear, dividing his attention between the compound to their left and behind and the dark structures ahead.

Directly in back of the lighthouse was what had to be the dormitory, a long, flat building almost twice the size of the concrete blocks they'd left behind. They hadn't come across quarters for the Umbrella workers anywhere else, and it had the look of a bunkhouse—designed for sleeping and eating, no thought given to aesthetic appeal. They probably should check it out, but David didn't want to waste a moment in their search for the lab.

The thought brought on another wave of guilt and angst that he tried unsuccessfully to block out. He needed to be effective, to get them to the laboratory as quickly as possible without floundering in his doubts and emotions—but all he kept thinking, kept *wishing* was that he'd been infected instead.

But you're not, some tiny part of him whispered, *Karen's got it and wishing is pointless. It won't cure her and it will cloud your ability to lead.*

David ignored the small voice, thinking instead of how badly he'd screwed them all. Who was he, to lead a fight against Umbrella, to clean up the S.T.A.R.S. and bring honor back to the job? He couldn't even keep his people safe, couldn't plan a simple covert op—couldn't even battle the demons of self-doubt and horrified guilt that raged inside of him.

They neared the lifeless dorm building, John slowing to let the rest of them catch up. David saw that his team was tired, but at least Karen didn't look any worse. In the gentle light of the swollen moon, she seemed pale and somehow fragile. The deathly pallor she'd worn beneath the fluorescents had translated into a soft, porcelain cast, the redness of her gaze turning to shadow. If he hadn't known better . . .

Ah, but you do. How long now, before that milky skin starts to peel, to flake away? How long before she can't be trusted with a weapon, before you have to restrain her from—

Stop it!

He let them catch their breath, turning to get a better look at the lighthouse less than twenty meters away—and felt his stomach clench, his heart shudder suddenly for no reason that he could have explained. It was an old lighthouse, a tall, cylindrical outdated building, weathered and dark and as seemingly deserted as the rest of the compound. Looking at it, he experienced the feeling he'd had earlier of impending doom, of options closing down behind them and the spinning wheel of darkness ahead.

"Come on," John said briskly, but David stopped him with a hand on his arm, shaking his head slowly.

Not safe. That tiny voice again, familiar yet strange.

He stared at the looming tower, feeling lost, feeling uncertain and out of control as the wind swept over them, the waves pounding the cliff. They were waiting. It wasn't safe, but they had to go in, they couldn't just stand there—

—and it hit him suddenly, a clear realization of what it was that had gone wrong in his mind. What was *really* wrong. It wasn't his competence, it wasn't his ability to think or plan or fight. It was something far worse, something he might have noticed much earlier if he hadn't let himself get so wrapped up with guilt.

I stopped trusting my instincts. Without the security of the S.T.A.R.S. behind me, I forgot to listen to that voice—so terrified of making a mistake that I lost my ability to hear, to know what to do. Every time the fear hit me, I pushed through it, I ignored it—and I made it that much stronger.

Even as he thought it, as he *believed* it, he felt the blackness of doubt lift from his exhausted thoughts. The guilt eased back, allowing a kind of clarity to filter through—and with it, the tiny voice inside took on a power that he'd almost forgotten it could have.

It's not safe, so hit the door fast, two in low, the rest high and covered outside—

All of this flashed through his mind in seconds. He turned to look at his team, watching him, waiting for him to lead. And for the first time in what felt like an eternity, he knew that he could.

"I think it's a trap," he said. "John, you and I go in low, I'll take west—Rebecca, I want you and Steve to stand on either side of the door and fire at anything standing; keep firing until we call clear. Sorry, Karen, you'll sit this one out."

They nodded all around and started for the deep shadows that surrounded the ominous tower, David in front, finally feeling as though he was doing something useful. Maybe that spinning destiny was too vast, moving too quickly for them to deny—but he wasn't going to let it run them over without at least putting up a fight.

Karen deserved that much. They all did.

Karen hung back as they moved into position, leaning against the back wall of the large building behind the lighthouse to watch. She felt winded by the climb up the hill, winded and strange and there was a buzzing in her brain that wouldn't go away, wouldn't let her fully concentrate. . . .

. . . *getting sick. Getting sicker, fast.*

It scared her, but somehow it wasn't as bad as it had been. In fact, it wasn't really that scary at all. The initial terror had gone, leaving her with only a memory of the adrenaline rush, like a whiff of a bad dream. The itch was distracting, but not exactly an itch anymore. What had felt like a million bug bites on her skin, each separate and distinct and screaming for relief, had—connected. It was the only way she could think to describe the sensation. They had connected, had become a thick blanket over her body that crawled and squirmed, as if her skin had come to life and was scratching itself. It was weird, but not exactly unpleasant—

"Now!"

At the sound of David's voice, Karen focused on the sudden action in front of her, the buzzing hum in her head making it all seem strange, speeded up somehow. The door to the lighthouse crashing open, David and John leaping into the blackness, bullets flashing and booming. The high, whining rattle of an M-16 inside. Steve and Rebecca, ducking and firing, out and in and out again, their bodies blurred by speed, their Berettas dancing like black metal birds.

It was happening so fast that it seemed to take a long, long time for it to stop. Karen frowned, wondering how that could be—

—and then saw David and John step back out into the blue light of the moon, and realized that she was happy to see them. Even with their strange and distorted faces, their long bodies that moved too quickly . . .

. . . what's happening to me . . .

Karen shook her head but the buzzing only seemed to get louder—and she was afraid again, afraid that David and John and Steve and Rebecca would leave her behind. They'd leave her behind and she wouldn't have anyone to, to—ease her mind. That was bad.

David was in front of her, staring at her with eyes like wet, dark cherries. "Karen, are you okay?"

At the look on his round and pointed face and the sound of softness in his voice, Karen felt happy again, and knew that she had to tell him the truth. With a tremendous effort, she found the strength to say what had to be said, her voice coming out of the crawling body and the buzzing, sounding as strange to her as the wind.

"It's getting worse now," she said. "I don't think right, David. Don't leave me."

John and Rebecca, their hot, hot hands touching her, leading her away and to the darkness of the open door. Her body worked, but her mind was clouded by the trembling buzzing hum. There were things she wanted to tell them, things that drifted through the cloud like flashes of pretty pictures—but the building they moved her to was dark and hot, and there was a body on the floor holding a rifle. His face, she could see. His face wasn't strange; it was white, white and curling, textured like the buzzing and the crawling. It was a face that made sense.

"I got the door," Steve said, looking up and grinning, white, white teeth. "One-three-five." There was a keypad next to an open hole, stairs leading down, and Steve's teeth disappeared, his flat face wrinkling.

"Karen—"

"We have to hurry."

"Hang on baby, hang on, we'll be there soon—"

Karen let them help her, wondering why their faces looked so strange, wondering why they smelled so hot and good.

FOURTEEN

ATHENS HAD FAILED.

Dr. Griffith stared at the blinking white light by the door, cursing Athens, cursing Lyle Ammon, cursing his luck. He hadn't told Athens how to get back inside, which could only mean that the intruders had made it past him. Ammon had left them a message or sent them one, it didn't matter—all that mattered was that they were coming and he had to assume that they had the key. He'd torn down the markers weeks ago, but perhaps they had directions, perhaps they'd find him and—

Don't panic, no need for panic. You prepared for this, simply move on, next plan. Division first, twofold effect—less firepower, bait for later . . . and a chance to see how well Alan can perform.

Griffith turned to Dr. Kinneson and spoke quickly,

keeping the instructions clear and simple, the route as easy as possible. Griffith had already worked out the questions they'd probably ask, though he knew there was a chance they'd try for more information. He gave Alan several random phrases to respond with, then gave him the small semi-automatic pistol from Dr. Chin's desk drawer, watching as Alan tucked it beneath his lab coat to make sure it was hidden. The bullet carrier was empty, but he didn't think it was possible to tell, not if the hammer was pulled back. He also gave Alan his key; a risk, but then the entire scenario was a risk. With the fate of the world resting in his hands, he'd take any chance necessary.

After Alan had gone, Griffith sat down in a chair to wait for a reasonable amount of time, his gaze wandering to the six stainless canisters in restless anticipation. His plans wouldn't fail; the righteousness of his work would see him through this invasion. If Alan was caught out, there were still the Ma7s, there was still Louis, there were still the syringes and his hiding place, the airlock controls in easy reach.

Past all of that, there was still the sunrise, waiting. Dr. Griffith smiled dreamily.

Karen could still walk, still seemed to understand at least part of what they were saying to her, but the few words she could manage didn't seem to relate to anything. As they'd gone down the stairs from the lighthouse, she'd said "hot" twice. As they'd walked into the wide, dank tunnel at the base of the steps, she'd said, "I don't want," an expression of fear on her deathly pale, searching face. Rebecca was terrified that even if they found a way to reverse the viral load, it would be too late.

It had all happened so suddenly, so fast that she could still hardly comprehend it. There'd been a man waiting for them in the darkness of the lighthouse, a trap just as David had intuited. As soon as they'd gone in, he'd opened fire with an automatic rifle, strafing the door from the shadows beneath the winding metal stairs. Thanks to David's plan, it had been over in seconds—and as Steve had discovered the access door and punched in the code, Rebecca and John had looked over their waiting attacker, had seen in the narrow beam of John's flashlight that the man had been infected—his paper-white skin was flaking and creased with strange, peeling etched lines. He'd looked somehow different than the Trisquad victims she'd seen, less decayed, his open, staring eyes somehow more human . . . but then David had gone to get Karen and Rebecca's interest had been suddenly and cruelly diverted.

It had been the walk up the hill, she'd decided. Even though it shouldn't have made a difference, she couldn't imagine what else might have brought on the amplification so quickly. Somehow, the T-Virus must have responded to the physiological changes of Karen's increased heart rate and circulation—but as they'd led the confused and stumbling woman into the lighthouse, Rebecca had found that she'd stopped caring about *how;* all she wanted was to get to the lab, to try and salvage what was left of Karen Driver's sanity.

The tunnel beneath the lighthouse seemed to lead back toward the compound in a curving, twisting trail, and was carved from the heavy limestone of the cliff. Mining lights were strung along the walls, casting strange shadows as they moved forward, silent and grimly afraid, John and Steve half-pulling Karen between them. Rebecca was last, again feeling a horrible sense of déjà vu as they stumbled along, remembering the tunnels beneath the Spencer estate. The same cold damp emanated from the stone, and she felt the same terrible feelings of moving toward unknown danger, exhausted and afraid of screwing up—of not being able to prevent a disaster.

The disaster has already happened, she thought helplessly, watching Karen struggle to keep walking. *We're losing her. In another hour, probably less, she'll be too far gone to ever come back.*

As it was, John and Steve shouldn't be touching her. In a single, easy movement she could get at either one of them, biting before they had a chance to let go. Even that concept made her sick with sorrow and an aching, heavy feeling of loss.

The tunnel veered to the left, and Rebecca realized they had to be incredibly close to the ocean; the walls seemed to tremble and shake from a muted thunder beyond, and the tunnel was thick with a damp and fishy smell. Parts of the floor seemed too smooth to have been created by human hands, and Rebecca wondered vaguely if the tunnel opened up ahead somewhere, perhaps had once been flooded by the sea—

"Bloody hell," David whispered angrily. "Shit."

Rebecca looked up. When she saw what was ahead, she felt her last flicker of hope for Karen die.

We'll never find it in time.

The tunnel *did* open up, a few hundred meters ahead of where David had stopped. It widened considerably, in fact—and was connected by five smaller tunnels, each branching off in a slightly different direction.

"Which way is southwest?" John asked anxiously. Karen leaned against him, her head rolling forward.

David's voice was still angry, frustration raising his words to an echo that bounced through the five stone corridors, circling back to fill the cavern.

"I don't *know,* I thought we were already headed southwest—and yet none of these is in direct alignment, and none head directly *east,* either."

They moved into the rough-hewn cavern, staring helplessly at the smooth tunnels, each of them strung with lights that disappeared around turns and bends. They had obviously been carved by water, perhaps had once been connected to the sea caves that David had originally meant for them to find. The tunnels weren't as wide as the one they stood in, but were wide enough to accommodate human passage comfortably enough, and at least three meters high. There was no way to guess which one was used to get to the lab—

—or if any of them lead to the lab, we don't even know for certain that it's down here. . . .

"If none of them goes east, then we have to pick the one that looks the most likely to go southwest," Steve said quietly. "Besides, east of here is water."

Karen mumbled something unintelligible, and Rebecca stepped forward worriedly to see how she was. Though John and Steve still steadied her, she seemed to have no trouble standing on her own.

Rebecca touched her clammy, sweating forehead and Karen's rolling eyes fixed on her, glassy and red, the pupils dilated.

"Karen, how are you doing?" she asked softly.

Karen blinked slowly. "Thirsty," she whispered, her voice bubbling and liquid sounding.

Still responsive, thank God. . . .

Rebecca touched her throat lightly, feeling the rapid, thready pulse beneath her fingers. It was definitely quicker than before, up in the lighthouse. Whatever the virus was doing to her, it wouldn't be much longer before Karen's body gave out.

Rebecca turned, feeling desperate and angry, wanting to scream for somebody to *do* something—

—and heard the pounding footsteps, echoing up through one of the tunnels. She grabbed for her Beretta, saw John and David do the same as Steve held onto Karen.

Which one, where's it coming from? Griffith? Is it Griffith?

The sound seemed to circle, coming from everywhere at once—and then Rebecca saw him, appearing from around a corner in the passage second from the right. A stumbling figure, a flapping, dusty lab coat—

—and then he saw them, and even from fifteen meters away, Rebecca could see the stunned and almost hysterical joy that swept across his face. The man ran for them, his short brown hair wild and disheveled, his eyes bright and lips trembling. He wasn't holding any kind of weapon, though Rebecca kept hers raised.

"Oh, thank God, thank God! You have to help me! Dr. Thurman, he's gone mad, we have to get out of here!"

He staggered out of the tunnel and nearly ran into David, apparently oblivious to the pistols trained on him as he babbled on.

"We have to go, there's a boat we can use, we have to get out before he kills us all—"

David shot a glance back, saw that Rebecca and John still had him covered. He tucked the Beretta into his side holster and stepped forward, taking the man's arm.

"Easy, calm down. Who are you, do you work here?"

"Alan Kinneson," the man gasped. "Thurman kept me locked up in the lab but he heard you coming and I managed to get away. But he's crazy. You have to help me get to the boat! There's a radio, we can call for help!"

The lab!

"Which way is the laboratory?" David asked quickly.

Kinneson didn't seem to hear him, too panicked by whatever he thought Thurman might do to them.

"The radio's on the boat, we can call for help and then get away!"

"The laboratory," David repeated. "Listen to me—did you just come from there?"

Kinneson turned and pointed to the tunnel that was next to the one he'd come from, the one in the middle. "The lab is that way—"

He pointed back the way he'd come. "—and the boat's down there. These caves are like a maze."

Though he seemed to have calmed slightly as he pointed to the tunnels, when he turned back to face them, he looked as hysterical as he had before. He seemed to be in his mid-thirties at first glance, but David noticed he had deep lines etched at the corners of his eyes and mouth and realized he had to be much older. Whoever he was and however old he was, he was caught in the grip of an almost mindless panic.

"The radio's on the boat, we can call for help and then get away!"

David's thoughts raced in time with his pounding heart. This was it, this was their chance—

—*we get to the lab, make this Thurman give us the cure and then get out of this place, before anyone else gets hurt*—

He turned to look at the others and saw the same hopeful looks that he knew he wore, John and Steve both nodding sharply. Rebecca didn't look as enthused. She jerked her head back, motioning for David to move out of Kinneson's earshot.

"Excuse us a moment," David said, forcing a politeness that he didn't feel. Kinneson was one of the researchers from Trent's list.

"We have to hurry!" The man babbled, but he didn't follow as David stepped back toward the others, the four of them leaning together to talk, Karen resting against Steve's arm.

Rebecca's voice was hushed and worried. "David, we can't take Karen to the lab if Griffith—if *Thurman* is there; what if we have to fight?"

John nodded, shooting a glance at the wild-eyed researcher. "And I don't think we should leave this guy alone, he's likely to take off with our ride home."

David frowned, thinking. Steve was a better shot, but John was stronger. If they had to force Thurman to give them the T-Virus cure, John could probably intimidate him more easily.

"We split up. Steve, you take Karen to the boat, keep an eye on Kinneson. We'll go to the lab, get what we need and then meet you there. Agreed?"

Tight nods, and then David turned, addressing Kinneson.

"We need to get to the laboratory, but our friend Karen isn't well. We'd like for you to take her and an escort to the boat, and wait for us."

Kinneson's eyes seemed to blank out for just a second, the strange, vacant look there and gone so quickly that David wasn't even sure he'd seen it.

"We have to hurry," he said quickly, then turned and started back down the passage he'd appeared from, walking at a brisk pace.

David felt a sudden worry, staring at Kinneson's rapidly receding back, his dirty lab coat floating out behind him.

He didn't even ask who we are. . . .

As Steve and Karen started to enter the tunnel, David touched Steve's arm, speaking softly. "Watch him carefully, Steve. We'll be there as soon as we can."

Steve nodded and moved off after the strange Dr. Kinneson, Karen stumbling along next to him.

John and Rebecca were already standing in front of the middle passageway, weapons still in hand. The chamber shook as outside, a muffled thunder roared.

Without speaking, the three of them started down the gloomy tunnel in a tired but determined jog, ready to face the human monster behind the many tragedies of Caliban Cove.

They turned the first corner, Karen hanging onto his shoulder with a cold and sweating hand—and the researcher was just rounding a bend farther ahead, a good hundred meters away. Steve caught a glimpse of fluttering white and the heel of a black loafer, and then he was out of sight, clattering footsteps moving away.

Great. Lost in a goddamn sea cave labyrinth because Dr. Strangelove has a schedule to keep—

Karen let out a low moan of soft distress and Steve

felt the cold, hard knot in his stomach clench tighter, his fear of getting lost nothing next to fear he felt for Karen. She was leaning on him more heavily, her feet dragging against the dank limestone floor.

David, John, Rebecca, please hurry, please don't let Karen get any worse—

He pulled her along as quickly as he could, concerned about catching up to Kinneson, worried about the others putting themselves in danger, afraid for the desperately sick woman who clung to his side. Except for meeting Rebecca, it had to be the worst day of his life. He'd only been with the S.T.A.R.S. for a year and a half, and while he'd been in threatening situations before, they didn't come close to what he'd experienced in the few short hours since they'd been knocked out of the raft.

Sea monsters, zombies with guns—and now Karen. Smart, serious Karen, losing her mind, maybe turning into one of those things. We're so close to getting out of here and it may still be too late. . . .

As they reached the turn in the tunnel, Steve realized that he couldn't hear Kinneson's footsteps anymore. He staggered around the corner, thinking that he should call for him to wait up, not to get too far ahead—

—and he stopped cold, his gut plummeting to somewhere around his knees. Kinneson stood two meters away, holding a .25 semi-automatic, his face and eyes as strangely blank and lifeless as a mannequin's. He stepped forward and pressed the small bore into Steve's stomach, hard, jerking the Beretta out of his holster and then stepping back. The flat-eyed doctor moved to one side, now holding both weapons on them as he motioned for Steve to move in front of him.

"Watch him carefully, Steve. . . ."

Steve held on to Karen's side, fumbling through his thoughts for ways to stall, to reason with Kinneson, his body tensing to spring even as his brain screamed at him to go along, not to get shot—

—*what would happen to Karen?*

"You will come to the lab," Kinneson said tonelessly, "or I'll kill you."

It was the inflectionless voice of a computer, coming from the blankly merciless face of a man who suddenly didn't seem human, not at all.

"We know what you did here," Steve spat. "We know all about your goddamn Trisquads, we know about the T-Virus, and if you want to get out of this without—"

"You will come to the lab or I'll kill you."

Steve felt a helpless shudder run through his body. Kinneson's tone hadn't altered at all, his gaze as fixed and emotionless as his voice. Steve noticed the lines then, the deep, spidering lines that swept away from his cold brown eyes, sat at the corners of his slack and expressionless lips.

Oh my God—

"You will come to the lab or I'll kill you," he repeated, and this time, he raised both weapons—holding them inches away from Karen's sagging head.

Steve knew she was dying, knew that there was a

good chance she'd lose against the virus and become a violent, insane creature before the night was through—

—*but I have to protect her for as long as I can. If I sacrificed her to save myself and there was even a chance that she could've been cured . . .*

Steve wouldn't, *couldn't* do it. Even if it meant his own life.

Holding Karen tightly, he stepped ahead of the thing and started to walk.

Enough time had passed. If the intruders had done what they were supposed to do, they would have split up, some of them heading mistakenly for the pen, some accompanying the good doctor back to the lab. If Alan had failed, he'd at least have stalled the intruders long enough to keep them out in the open. Either way, it was time.

Griffith tapped the control panel for the Ma7 enclosure, thinking wistfully how much fun it would be to see the looks on their faces. The red light flashed to green, signifying that the gate was fully open.

No matter, he supposed. So long as they died.

Fifteen

THE WINDING TUNNEL SEEMED TO GO ON forever. Every time they rounded a turn, Rebecca expected to see a sealed door, a slot set next to it for the key card that David carried. As the corners continued, the hanging lights going on for another stretch of tunnel, each as empty and featureless as the stretch before, she stopped wishing for the door. A sign would suffice, an arrow painted on the wall, a chalk mark—*anything* that would put to rest her growing suspicion that they'd been misled.

Lied to by an Umbrella scientist? Perish the thought. . . .

Tired sarcasm aside, Kinneson had been weird, but had definitely seemed frightened to the point of hysteria. Could he have been confused in his panic, pointed to the wrong passage? Or was the lab just better hidden than they thought?

Or did he send us off on a snipe hunt, some dead-end cave—or even a trap, something dangerous, meant to keep us out of the way while he . . .

While he did something to Steve and Karen. The thought frightened her even more than the concept of walking into a trap. Karen was desperately ill, she wouldn't be able to defend herself, and Steve—

No, Steve's okay. He'd be able to take Kinneson in a heartbeat—

Except that Karen was with him. A very sick Karen, struggling just to stay upright.

Their jog had slowed to a shag, David and John both breathing heavily, frowns deepening across their exhausted faces. David held up a hand, stopping them.

"I don't think it's this way," he panted. "We should have seen something by now. And the piece of paper with the key card said southwest, east—I'm not sure, but I think after that last turn, we're heading west."

John bobbed his head, his short, tight hair glistening with sweat. "I don't know which way we're going, but I *know* I think Kinneson's full of shit. The guy works for Umbrella, for chrissake."

"I agree," Rebecca said, breathing deeply. "I think we should go back. We have to get to the lab, soon. I don't think—"

Clank!

They froze, staring at each other. From somewhere

farther down the endless tunnel, something made of heavy metal had just been moved.

"The lab?" Rebecca said hopefully. "Could it—"

A low, strange sound cut her off, the words dying in her throat as the noise picked up strength. It was like nothing she'd ever heard before—a dog howling, combined with an off-key whistling whine and the sound of a newborn baby's desperate cry. It was a lonely, terrible sound, rising and falling through the tunnel, finally building to a warbling, mournful shriek—

—then it was joined by several others.

She was suddenly absolutely certain that she didn't want to see what was making that sound, even as David started backing up, his face pale and eyes wide.

"Run," he said, training his Beretta on the empty passage ahead of them, waiting until they had stumbled past before turning to follow.

Rebecca felt a burst of incredible energy as adrenaline gushed into her body, sent her sprinting through the shadowy tunnel to escape the rising shrieks of whatever was behind them. John was just in front of her, his muscled arms and legs pumping madly, and she could hear the clattering steps of David on her heels.

The howls were getting louder, and Rebecca could *feel* the stone vibrate beneath her flying feet, the heavy, galloping steps of the shrieking beasts thundering after them.

—not gonna make it—

Even as she realized that they'd be overtaken, she heard David gasp out, "Next turn—"

—and as they reached the end of the empty stretch where the tunnel curved again, Rebecca whirled around, raising the Beretta in her sweating, shaking hand, training it back on the last turn they'd taken. John and David flanked her, gasping, nine-millimeters aimed alongside hers. Twenty meters of blank passage, filled with the now deafening cries of their unseen pursuers.

As the first of them tore into view, all three of them fired, slugs ripping into the creature that at first Rebecca thought was a lioness—then a giant lizard—then a dog. She caught only a mad, patchwork vision of the impossible thing, seeing parts of it that her mind fit into a whole—the slitted, cat-like pupils. The giant snake head, a gaping, slavering jaw filled with bladed teeth. The squat and powerful barrel-chested body, sand-colored, thick legs bowing in front, muscular, springing haunches propelling it toward them at an incredible speed—

—and even as the bullets found its strange, reptilian flesh, there was another behind it—

—and the first explosive rounds that smacked into the thick body of the closest creature knocked it off of its clawed feet, staggered it backward as blooms of watery blood spattered the tunnel walls—

—and, shaking its head, screaming in ferocious sorrow, it launched itself at them again.

—*oh shit*—

Rebecca squeezed the trigger again, four, five, six,

her mind screaming as loudly as the two monstrous animals that ran at them, eight, nine, ten—

—and the first went down, stayed down, but there was still the second and now a third, tearing down the tunnel, and the Beretta only held fifteen rounds—

We're gonna die—

David jumped back, behind the line of thundering fire. An empty clip skittered across the floor, and then he was next to her again, aiming and squeezing, the Beretta jerking smoothly in his practiced hand.

Rebecca counted her last round and stumbled backward, praying that she could do it as fast as David—

—and saw that the third animal was stumbling back, its wide chest gushing thin streamers of red. It collapsed into the puddle of watery fluid it created and stayed there.

Nothing in the tunnel moved, but there were at least two more around the corner. Their wailing cries continued to wax and wane through the tunnel, but they stayed back, out of sight—as if they knew what had happened to their siblings, and were too smart to charge into waiting death.

"Fall back," David said hoarsely, and still aiming at the blind corner, they started to edge backward, the shrieks of the hybrid creatures rolling over them in lonely, terrible waves.

Griffith moved quickly away from the door when he heard the key in the lock, not wanting to be too close to whomever Alan had brought along. He had Thurman already standing ready, just in case there were any sudden moves—but when he saw the young man and his passive partner step into the lab, he doubted he'd have any trouble.

What's this? A few too many drinks, perhaps? An unseen mortal wound?

Griffith smiled, waiting for him to speak or for the woman to move, his heart full and warm with good humor. It had been so long since he'd talked to someone who could respond without prompting, and the fact that his fine plan had worked made him all the merrier. Behind him, Alan sealed the door and stood blankly, holding two weapons on the unlikely pair.

The young man gazed wide-eyed around the laboratory, his dark gaze settling on the wide airlock window in something like awe. The woman's head was down, rolling across her chest.

He had the deep, natural tan of a Hispanic, or perhaps someone from India. Not too tall, but sturdy enough. Yes, he'd do quite nicely . . . and since this might even have been the one to destroy Athens, there was a certain poetic justice being served.

The youth's darting gaze finally rested on Griffith, curious and not altogether as frightened as Griffith would have liked.

We'll see about that. . . .

"Where are we?" the young man asked quietly.

"You are in a chemical research laboratory, approximately twenty meters below the surface of Caliban Cove," Griffith said. "Interesting, yes? Those clever designers even built it inside of a shipwreck—or they built the shipwreck around the lab, I forget ex—"

"Are you Thurman?"

Such manners!

Griffith smiled again, shaking his head. "No. That fat, hopeless creature standing to your left is Dr. Thurman. I am Nicolas Griffith. And you might be . . . ?"

Before the young man could speak, the woman rolled her head up, a wobbling white face looking around in fixed, helpless hunger.

An infected one!

"Thurman, take the woman and hold her," Griffith said quickly. He couldn't have her damaging the fine specimen Alan had managed to catch—

—but as Thurman grabbed for the female, the young man resisted, pushing at Louis with fast, angry hands, a sneer of bravado on his face.

Griffith felt a pulse of distress. "Alan, hit him!"

Dr. Kinneson brought his hand up quickly, cracking the struggling youth a smart blow across the back of his skull; he stopped fighting just long enough for Thurman to pull the woman away.

"She's *gone,*" Griffith said forcefully, wondering why on earth anyone would want to hang on to one of *those.* "Look at her, can't you see she's not human anymore? She's one of Birkin's puppets, one of the pathetically altered hungry. A zombie. A Trisquad unit without training."

Even as Griffith spoke, a fascinating turn of events

took place. The woman squirmed around in Thurman's grasp—and with one quick movement, darted forward and bit into Louis's face. She pulled back with a thick, bloody mouthful of his cheek and started to chew enthusiastically.

"Karen, oh my God, *no*—"

For as upset as he sounded, the young man didn't move to do anything about it. For that matter, neither did Louis. The doctor stood calmly, blood pouring down his face, watching the T-Virus drone lustily swallow the piece of tender flesh. Griffith was transfixed.

"Look at that," he said softly. "Not a grimace of pain, not a flutter of emotion . . . smile, Louis!"

Thurman grinned even as the woman lunged forward again, managing to snag his protruding lower lip. With a wet, tearing sound, the lip ripped away, exposing an even wider grin. Blood gushed. The woman chewed.

Amazing. Absolutely breathtaking.

The young man was quivering, his deep tan undershot with a sickly pallor. He didn't seem to appreciate what he was seeing, and Griffith realized that he probably wouldn't; the woman must have been a friend.

Too bad. Pearls before swine . . .

"Alan, take hold of our young man, and hold him tightly."

The youth didn't struggle, too absorbed in the apparent horror that he was experiencing. The female got another piece of cheek, and Louis's smile wavered, probably from muscle trauma.

As much as Griffith wanted to continue watching, there was work to be done. The young man's other friends might manage to put down the Ma7s—and if they succeeded with that, they might come looking for their bright young man.

But by then, he'll be my *bright young man. . . .*

Griffith walked to a counter and picked up a measured syringe, tapping the side of it with one finger. He turned to the silent guest, wondering if he should reveal his brilliant scheme for catching his friends. Wasn't that what "villains" always did in movies? He considered it only briefly, then decided against it; he'd always considered it a foolish plot point. And he was far from villainous. It was *they* who had invaded his sanctuary, threatened his plans for creating worldwide peace. There was no question who the evildoers were in this story.

The young Hispanic was still watching the bizarre luncheon, his mouth literally hanging open in dismay; Karen was swallowing Thurman's nose, and making quite a mess. He'd have to dispose of her before Louis's arms gave out, though that gave him plenty of time.

Stepping forward quickly, Griffith jabbed the needle into the youth's burly arm and depressed the plunger.

Only then did he struggle, his shocked gaze turning to Griffith, his body twisting and flailing. One of

Alan's arms seemed to give a little, but he had a good, tight hold on the fighting Hispanic.

Griffith smiled into his face, shaking his head. "Relax," he said soothingly. "In just a few moments, you won't feel a thing."

Slowly, too slowly, they backed toward the chamber they'd started in, the lizard-creatures following, careful not to step into view, screaming their terrible song. John kept thinking of Karen and Steve, led off to God knew where by the Umbrella doc, and wished desperately that the monsters would just charge. He felt the moments slipping by, moments that may have already cost Karen her only chance, moments in which Steve might be fighting for his life—

Come on, you stupid shits! We're right here, free lunch! Come on!

They'd tried yelling, tried firing and stamping their feet, but the creatures wouldn't take the bait. Once, David had tried to fake them out, the three of them slipping back around a corner—and when the big lizards had skulked through the tunnel after them, they'd jumped back around and started blasting. John got a single round into one of them, and they'd seen that there were only two of the beasts left—but both had gotten to cover before any serious damage had been done, and hadn't fallen for the ploy again.

"Sly bastards," John snarled for about the twentieth time, backing up as quickly as he could. "What the hell are they waiting for?"

Neither Rebecca nor David answered, since they'd already discussed it, talking over the creeping shrieks of the stalking monsters. They were waiting for the three of them to turn around.

After what felt like an eternity of slow motion, of backing through the empty tunnel one sliding step at a time, they heard the distant, familiar sound of the cavernous chamber they'd left—muffled waves and thundering vibrations as background to the echoing howls.

Thank God, thank God, how long? Fifteen, twenty minutes?

"When we get into the open, flank the tunnel," David said tightly. "I'm going to turn and run, draw them out—"

Rebecca shook her head, her young features pinched with worry. "You're a better shot than I am, and I can run faster. I should do it."

They had almost reached the chamber. John shot a glance at David, could see him struggling with the decision—and finally he nodded, sighing.

"Right. Run as fast as you can, back for the stairs to the lighthouse. We'll pick them off as soon as they're too far along to turn around."

Rebecca blew out sharply. "Got it. Just say when."

John could feel the change in the air just behind him, the drafts that swirled around the underground chamber fluttering against the back of his neck. Another step and they were surrounded by open space.

John quickly side-stepped, standing between the

tunnel they'd just backed out of and the one next to it. He saw David get into position, Rebecca standing perfectly still in the mouth of the passage—

"Go!"

Rebecca spun and ran, sprinting away, and John tensed, Beretta held close to his face, listening for the rising shrieks, the pound of feet—

"Now!" David shouted, and they both swung into the passage, firing.

Crack-crack-crack-crack!

The howling monsters were less than six meters away and the heavy rounds smashed into them, great, bloody holes exploding through their rubbery skin, bone and watery red splattering wildly.

The shrieks died beneath the thundering bullets, neither of the reptilian things making it as far as the opening. Two strange bodies fell still, crumpling to the stone floor in ragged heaps.

As soon as they stopped firing, Rebecca came jogging back into the chamber, her cheeks flushed, her eyes flashing with urgency.

"Let's go," David said, and then the three of them were running into the passage that Kinneson had disappeared into, the lost time lending a desperation to their flight.

John finally let the fear slip inside, giving up the angry frustration he'd suffered through their backward crawl.

Karen, be okay. Please, don't let anything have happened to her, Lopez—

The tunnel turned, angled down, the three of them

curving with it, terror for their friends and teammates driving them faster. John swore to himself that if they were all right, if there was still time for Karen, if they could all make it out of this alive, he'd give anything.

My car, my house, my money, I won't screw anyone else till I get married, I'll clean up my act and walk the straight and narrow—

It wasn't enough, and he didn't know why anyone would want it—but he'd sacrifice anything, do whatever it took.

The passage swerved again, still sliding down and they tore around the corner—

—and there was a wide open set of doors, a tiny passage between the outer and inner, a giant and dimly lit room behind it. Steve leaned against the frame, holding his Beretta, his face pale and blank.

"Steve! What happened, what—" David started, but the look on Steve's face as he turned to watch them approach, the terrible emptiness there, made them all stop in their tracks. Even as his mind searched to deny it, John's heart filled with a horrible, aching loss.

"Karen's dead," Steve said softly, then turned and walked into the room.

Sixteen

OH, NO. . . .

Rebecca felt a welling rush of sadness inside as she stared after Steve, John and David both grim and silent beside her. The blank shock on Steve's face before he'd turned away told them what must have happened.

Poor Karen. And Steve, what must it have been like . . .

They'd found the lab too late. She glanced down at the key card slot next to the door as she stepped into the double seal, feeling a horrible sense of futility at the pointlessness of it all. They'd come to find information, only to find tests, only for Karen to get infected—and then to turn against Steve even as they'd reached the one chance they might have had to cure her . . .

. . . but Kinneson. Thurman—

She stepped through the second door, frowning. The laboratory was huge, counters lined with equipment, desks piled incredibly high with stacks of paper—but it was the open hatch across from them that first commanded her attention, her gaze immediately drawn to the thick sheet of plexi or reinforced glass set into the thick door.

It was an airlock, the inner door standing open. And behind the second sealed door, past a mesh grate, the dark waters of the ocean swirled past, bubbles spinning by. The laboratory was underwater.

The second thing she noticed was the blood, a thick trail of crimson leading across the concrete floor in splatters and pools, but ending in a sliding smear. Steve must have moved a body—

—so much! God, not Karen's . . .

Steve had walked to the airlock and turned, seemed to be waiting for them to cross the room. Rebecca started toward him, her throat tight with sympathy and swelling tears. John and David were right behind her, quiet, looking around the vast room—

—when behind them, the door back into the passage slammed shut.

They spun around, saw Kinneson standing there, holding a tiny semi-automatic, a .25, pointing it at them with no expression on his face.

"Drop your weapons."

The low, quiet voice was Steve's.

Rebecca turned again, confused—and saw Steve pointing his Beretta at them, his face as blank as

Kinneson's. Now that she was close enough to the airlock, she saw the body on the grated floor. It was Karen, her white face streaked with blood, a gaping blackness where her left eye had been.

Oh, my God, what's going on—

David stepped toward him, holding his Beretta loosely, confusion and disbelief in his voice. "Steve, what are you doing? What's happened?"

"Drop your weapons," Steve said again. His voice had no emotion at all.

"What did you do to him?!"

John screamed, turned and fired at Kinneson, the round punching neatly through his left temple. Kinneson crumpled, sagging—

Boom!

The second shot came from Steve's Beretta, hitting John in the lower back. Blood gushed from the hole and as he staggered halfway around, Rebecca saw the dark fluid trickling from his mouth, the dazed disbelief in his eyes—

—and John crashed to the cement, spasming once before he lay motionless. It had all happened in the space of a few seconds.

"Drop your weapons," Steve said calmly. He pointed his semi at Rebecca.

For a moment, Rebecca could do nothing at all. She stared at Steve in horror, felt tears slipping down her frozen cheeks, unable to comprehend what had happened.

"Disarm," David said quietly, letting his slip from his fingers and clatter to the floor.

Rebecca dropped the Beretta, the heavy weapon falling from her equally heavy fingers.

"Back up," Steve said, still aiming at her chest.

"Do as he says," David said, his voice trembling just slightly.

They stepped back slowly, Rebecca unable to take her eyes from Steve's face, the handsome, boyish face she'd grown to care about. Now it was only a mask, worn by a . . .

. . . *by a zombie.*

They backed into a desk and stopped, watching dully as Steve moved to pick up their weapons, Rebecca's mind whirling with more than just horror and loss. A zombie that could walk and talk like a man. Like Kinneson. Like Steve.

How? When did this happen?

As Steve stepped away, a pleasant male voice came out of the corner of the room, from behind a desk.

"All finished, then? My God, what a Greek tragedy. . . ."

The voice was followed by an appearance. A slender, gray-haired man stood up and walked around the desk, moving almost casually to stand by Steve. He was in his mid-fifties, his hair long enough to brush at the collar of his lab coat, his lined face sporting a beaming smile.

"I'll repeat my instructions for the benefit of our guests," the man said happily. "If either of them makes any sudden moves, shoot them."

Rebecca knew who he was immediately, knew that she hadn't been wrong after all.

"Dr. Griffith," she said quietly.

Griffith arched an eyebrow, seeming amused. "My reputation precedes me! How did you know?"

"I've heard about you," she said coldly. "Or Nicolas Dunne, anyway."

His smile froze, then widened again. "All in the past," he said dismissively, waving one hand in the air. "And you'll never have a chance to tell anyone about the pleasure of our acquaintance, I'm afraid."

Griffith's smile faded, his dark blue gaze turning icy. "You people have held me up long enough. I'm tired of this game, so I believe that I'm going to have your nice young man kill you. . . ."

He brightened suddenly, and Rebecca saw the madness flashing in those eyes, the complete break from sanity.

"Now that I think of it, why create even more of a mess? Steve, tell our friends to get into the airlock, if you would be so kind."

Steve kept his weapon trained on her heart.

"Get into the airlock," he said calmly.

Before David could take a step, Rebecca started talking, fast and deadly serious.

"Was it the T-Virus? Did you use that as a platform for whatever this is? I know you were responsible for the increase in amplification time, but this is something new, this is something that Umbrella doesn't even know about. It's a mutagen with an instantaneous membrane fusion, isn't it?"

Griffith's eyes widened. "Steve, wait . . . what do you know about membrane fusion, little girl?"

"I know that you've perfected it. I know that you've managed to create a rapid fuse virion that apparently infects the brain tissue in under an hour—"

"In under *ten minutes,*" Griffith said, his whole demeanor changing from that of a smiling old man to that of a fanatic, his gaze narrowing with a dangerously brilliant intensity, his lips drawing tight over clenched teeth.

"These stupid, stupid animals with their ridiculous T-Virus! Birkin may have a mind, but the rest of them are *fools,* playing with war games while I've created a miracle!"

He turned, gesturing at a row of shining oxygen tanks next to the lab's entrance. "Do you know what that is, do you know what I've managed to synthesize? Peace! Peace and the freedom from choice for all of mankind!"

David felt his heart start to pound viciously, his entire body breaking out in a cold sweat. Griffith was pacing in front of them now, his eyes burning with mad genius.

"There's enough of my strain, of my creation in those tanks to infect a billion people in less than twenty-four hours! I've managed to find the answer, *the* answer to the pitiful, selfish, and self-important breed that the human race has become—when I give my gift to the wind, the world will become *free* again, it will be reborn, a simple and beautiful place for every creature, great and small, surviving on instinct alone!"

"You're insane," David breathed, knowing that Griffith could kill them, was *going* to kill them, but unable to stop himself from saying it. "You're out of your bloody mind!"

This is why my team is dead, why all those people are dead. He wants to turn the world into things like Kinneson. Like Steve.

Griffith snarled at him, flecks of spittle flying from his lips. "And you're *dead*. You're not going to be here when my miracle graces this earth, I, I—*deprive* you of my gift, both of you! When the sun comes up tomorrow, there will be peace, and neither of you will ever know a *second* of it!"

He whirled around, pointing at Steve. "Put them in the airlock, now!"

Steve raised the Beretta again, motioning toward the opened hatch, where Karen's lifeless body lay slumped and bloody on the floor.

He's out of reach, can't grab the weapon in time—

"Steve, *now!* Kill them if they won't go!"

David and Rebecca stepped into the lock, David's body cold, tensed, he had to *do* something or the world would be infected by this maniac's psychotic dream—

Steve slammed the lock closed.

They were trapped.

SEVENTEEN

GRIFFITH WAS FURIOUS, SHAKING WITH ANGER as the airlock door slammed closed. Didn't they *see*, didn't they understand anything but their own petty, stupid lives?

He stared at the young Steve, the rage spilling out, threatening to drive him insane, to make him vomit, to *kill*—

"Put that gun in your ugly face and pull the trigger, die, die, just *die!*"

Steve raised the weapon.

Rebecca screamed, beating her fists helplessly against the thick metal door.

No no no no no—
BOOM!

The thunder of the shot cut her screams off. Steve

fell against the base of the hatch, mercifully out of sight.

Already dead, he was already dead, it wasn't Steve anymore—

"Jesus . . ." David whispered, and Rebecca looked up, looked straight into Griffith's wildly petulant gaze through the window—

—and Griffith smiled suddenly, a beaming, triumphant grin of accomplishment and malicious spite. The raging loss and terror she felt were transformed by the sight of that smile. Rebecca stared into those raving blue eyes and realized that she'd never truly felt hate before.

Oh you miserable bastard—

He'd told them of his plan, but at that second, the thought was too big for her to fathom, too vast and insane a tragedy for her to fit her mind around. All she could think of was that he'd killed Karen and John, he'd killed Steve—and she wanted nothing more than to destroy him, to see him *lose,* to see him suffer and feel pain and—

—*and if we don't do something his madness will be fully realized and we have to stop it, to stop* him *from dancing on the grave of the world.*

Griffith moved to a control panel next to the door and started to press buttons, still smiling. There was a heavy *clanking* from the grated floor and water started to gurgle in, drawn from the icy black waters of the cove that pressed against the outer hatch. The airlock was just big enough for her and David not to have to stand on Karen's bloody, twisted body, and already the water was turning red, foaming up from an unseen vent and lapping at their feet, covering Karen's white fingers.

A minute, maybe less. . . .

In the lab, Griffith was leaning against a desk across from them, arms folded smugly, watching. Behind him, a backdrop of death—Kinneson, John, and the gleaming steel cylinders filled with Griffith's evil genius.

We have to do something!

Rebecca turned desperately to David, praying that he had some brilliant plan—and saw only resignation and sorrow in his eyes as he stared down at Karen's corpse, his shoulders slumped with defeat.

"David—"

He looked up at her bleakly, hopelessly. "I'm sorry," he whispered. "All my fault. . . ."

Karen's hands were already floating, tendrils of short blond hair haloing around her pitiful face. Rebecca grabbed at the latch of the door uselessly, felt its unmoving strength, sealed by Griffith's controls. Cold water seeped through the canvas of her shoes, over her ankles, the rising smells of salt and darkness and blood frightening her as badly as David's hopeless whispering drone.

"If I hadn't been so selfish . . . Rebecca, I'm so sorry, you have to believe that I never meant—"

Terrified, on the edge of hysteria, she grabbed his shoulders roughly, shouting. "Okay, fine, you're an asshole, but if Griffith releases that virus, millions of people are gonna *die!*"

For a second, she didn't think he'd heard her and

she felt the water rising, inching up her calves, her heart pounding wildly—and then his dark eyes sharpened, losing their glassy sheen. He looked quickly around the tight compartment, and she could see his mind working, see the sharp gaze taking in all of the details. Steel, watertight hatches; a mesh enclosure over the outer door, like a thin shark cage, two feet deep; cold water bubbling, over her knees now, Karen's arms and head lifting, floating—

"Doors are steel, the window's two inches of plexi—once the outer hatch pops, there's the cage—"

He looked into her eyes, his own filled with frustrated anger, with shock and apology—and shook his head.

She dropped her hands, her body starting to shiver from the cold, her thoughts delving into black despair. David sloshed closer and put his arms around her.

"Just your luck to meet me," he said softly, rubbing her upper arms as her teeth started to chatter, as the water swirled up around her hips, as Karen's lifeless hand brushed her leg—

Luck. Karen.

Rebecca's heart seemed to stop in mid-beat.

David held her tightly, wishing a million things, knowing that it was too late for any of them. He glanced into the lab and saw that Griffith was still watching them, still smiling. He looked away, filled with a useless, dismal hatred as the icy water slopped against his hips.

Murdering bloody bastard—

Rebecca tensed against his chest suddenly. She pushed away from him and grabbed at Karen's body, her fingers searching frantically through the dead woman's vest. She laughed, a bright, hysterical snap of joy—

—*she's gone mad*—

—and jerked a dark, round object from one of Karen's pockets. David saw what it was and felt pure amazement sweep through him.

"She carried it for luck," Rebecca chattered out quickly. "It's live."

David took the grenade and held it behind his back, his thoughts racing again, assessing, the water to his waist and almost to Rebecca's heaving chest.

—*outer door pops, pull the pin and get in the cage, hold the hatch closed*—

They'd probably still die. But if they could pull it off, they wouldn't go out alone.

Griffith watched the water rise, watched the two run through a stereotypical melodrama almost absently—his thoughts had already turned to the coming dawn, and the problem of getting the heavy canisters upstairs. He supposed it served him right, losing his temper that way. . . .

The pair were putting on quite a show. The girl, angry at the Brit's apathy; the quick, desperate look for a way out of their predicament. The final embrace, then the panic—the girl clutching at the T-Virus drone, the Brit talking at her, frowning, worried for her sanity even as the dark water rose over her young bosom.

Sad, so sad. They should never have come, never have tried to, to get at me. . . .

Now the man was holding her up, pathetically

working to postpone the inevitable as the water spun up across the glass. Once they were dead, he'd pop the cage, give the Leviathans a treat before setting them free again, free to swim in unmanned seas and live out their days in peace.

Ocean and land as one, his mind murmured dreamily. *Mirrors of simplicity, instinct . . .*

The drone body fluttered lazily past the window, and he saw that the two invaders had propped themselves between the hatches, struggling to hold on to the last bit of air. A determined pair, if thick-headed. It occurred to him suddenly that he'd never bothered to find out who they were, who had sent them . . .

. . . and it doesn't matter now, does it?

The lock had filled. The light on the control panel indicated that the outer door had unlatched. It was over—

—except they were scrambling to get out, kicking through into the cage, and something small dropped past the window as they pushed the door closed behind them—

Griffith frowned and—

BOOM!

He just had time to register disbelief before the hatch slammed into his body and the screaming torrent of liquid ice took his breath away.

Eighteen

WHEN THE GRENDADE EXPLODED, EVERY-
thing happened too fast for Rebecca to think about.
There were only sensations, terror reigning over all.

Brilliant light and explosive movement as the door
blew outward, hardness against her back that gave
way in an instant, lungs screaming, a billion bubbles
like bullets, and incredible, impossible pressure that
seemed to go on and on in shades of cold and black.
Faster than fast, movement and muffled, strange
sound.

Dark shapes moved over her feeling mind, blotting
out everything in growing flickers of dizziness and
her chest was imploding, her lungs eating themselves. She kicked and kicked and kicked and as her
legs started to weaken, the dark flickers swallowing
her up—

—air, sweet, wonderful air slapped across her dying face. She drank convulsively, gasping in great, heaving gulps of the stuff, still not thinking at all. Her body thought instead, greedily swallowing life, the spray and sting of salt, the warmer, rocking waves, a high, reedy buzz—

CRASH!

A massive wave of pressure pushed her forward, driving water up her nose as buckets of it suddenly rained down on top of her.

Rebecca gasped air, spinning, her mind connected to her body again.

David! What's—

"Rebecca!" A choked cry, from somewhere in the buzzing dark. The buzz was clearer now, it was—

CRASH!

Another surging wave, another torrent pouring over her, seeking to drown her as Griffith had been unable to do, and as the rain fell away, she saw light—thick beams of it piercing the dark, wild surface of the cove.

A boat. An engine's powerful, deepening thrum as it sped toward her over the thrashing sea.

"Rebecca!" David's desperate call, from her left.

"I'm here—"

CRASH!

She could see the explosion this time, see the giant column of water silhouetted against the searching beams of light before the debris-encrusted wave knocked her back, blinding her with a vicious slap of foam. She managed to take a quick gulp of air before the column came down, crashing over her, spattering loudly against the choppy surface.

Depth charges, they're firing depth charges— Umbrella?

The boat was less than thirty meters away when the engine suddenly cut out, the lights playing across the water in front of her. There was a splashing movement nearby—

—and the lights moved, one of the blindingly bright beams finding David's exhausted, dripping face a short distance away.

A man's voice, coming from the boat now moving slowly toward them. "This is Captain Blake of the Philadelphia S.T.A.R.S.! Identify yourself!"

S.T.A.R.S.?

Blake went on, his shout louder as the boat came closer. "The water's not safe! We're coming to get you out!"

David called back, his voice clogged and cracking. "Trapp, David Trapp, Exeters, and Rebecca Chambers—"

When Blake shouted again, he said the most wonderful, most beautiful words that Rebecca had ever heard.

"Burton sent us to find you! Hang on!"

Barry. Oh, thank God, Barry!

As drained as she was, as spiritually wasted, torn by loss and fear from the long, terrible night, Rebecca had just enough strength to smile.

That's when she heard the choking groan behind her.

There was darkness, tinged with red and an echo of pain. In that darkness, there was no self and no peace; he was alone and engaged in battle, a furious struggle to find the end to that absence of light. He knew that finding the end quickly was important, but a maze of strange and somehow frightening images blocked his way, insisting that he didn't need to hurry. A ghost, a soldier, a rage. The ringing laugh of a woman he had known who was no more—and the terrible dead eyes that had taken away the light in an explosion of fire and sound. Eyes that he knew but was afraid to remember. . . .

The maze beckoned him, called to him to explore deeper and give up his search for the end of darkness—that the path would only lead to greater pain—and he'd almost decided to stop fighting, to let the shadows take over when the light found *him* in an explosive blast of deafening thunder.

Then he was being shot through ice and liquid black, pounded to consciousness by pain—and it was the pain that he focused on in that screaming, terrible ride, the pain that drove him to fight the darkness. His awareness spun away as the air curdled in his lungs and the raging cold numbed the pain—but then he could breathe, and the jagged piece of bobbing wood beneath his clawed fingers told him that there was, in fact, light. He wasn't dead, although he almost wished he were—he could still hardly breathe, and the pain in his back was exquisite—and then he heard the sound of David's voice amidst the sloshing cold and felt that life might be worth living, after all.

He tried to call out, but all that emerged was an exhausted moan. There was a stab of sharp and blinding light—and then darkness again, but there was a flicker of awareness this time that allowed him to understand what was happening. Pain and movement, a feeling of weightless suspension and then hardness against his cheek. Chill and more movement, the sound of cloth ripping and paper tearing. Excited voices calling orders, and again, the shriek of torn flesh. When he came around again, he saw a shadow in a S.T.A.R.S. vest bending over him with an IV bag in one hand and a needle in the other.

Hope that's morphine, he tried to say, but again, he only groaned.

A split second later, he saw two pale blurs hovering over him as the S.T.A.R.S. shadow continued to work over him with warm and gentle hands. The blurs were David and Rebecca, eyes circled with dark, hair dripping, faces tired and lost.

"You're going to be okay, John," David said softly. "Just rest now. It's all over."

A spreading warmth started to flush through his body, a delicious, sleepy warmth that banished the roar of pain to a distant and faraway land. Just as a friendly darkness came to claim him, he looked into David's eyes and managed to rasp out what he suddenly wanted to say more than anything. It took great effort, but it had to be said.

"You two look like somethin' a coyote ate and shit off a cliff," he mumbled. "Seriously . . ."

John was followed into the healing blackness by the sweet sound of laughter.

The middle-aged S.T.A.R.S. medic had taken John inside the small cabin on the thirty-foot boat, coming out only once to tell them that everything looked all right. Two broken ribs, some deep tissue trauma and a punctured lung, but they'd managed to patch him up well enough to call him stable and he was resting comfortably. A medevac helicopter had already been radioed for and would be arriving soon, and the medic seemed confident that John would manage a full recovery. David had wept a little at the news, and not been a bit ashamed.

They sat in the back of the boat, huddled under a scratchy wool blanket as Blake and his team continued to set charges, powering easily back and forth across the cove. The Pennsylvania team had already brought up four of the giant creatures before they'd seen the explosive burst of air and debris that had come up from the lab, and it was starting to look as though there weren't any more.

David had one arm around Rebecca, the girl leaning against his chest as the black sky gradually started to shade to a deep, ethereal blue. Neither of them spoke, too tired to do more than watch the team work, dropping charges and searching the results, back and forth and back again. Blake had promised to send divers down for Griffith's tanks as soon as the cove was clear and John had been picked up. There were two wetsuits already laid out on the bow's deck, a young Alpha, whose name David had forgotten, prepping them with studied intensity. He reminded David of Steve a little bit. . . .

Somehow, the thought of Steve didn't bring the kind of pain that David expected it would. It hurt, it hurt like hell—Karen and Steve, gone—but when he thought of what they had managed to stop, what they had been a part of . . .

. . . it wasn't all for nothing. We stopped Griffith's insanity, stopped him from effectively killing millions of innocent people. God, they would have been so proud. . . .

The pain was bad, but the guilt wasn't as devastating as he'd feared it would be. His responsibility in their deaths was something he knew he'd have to ponder for a long time to come—but he thought that there was a good chance that he'd be able to find a way to come to terms with it eventually. He wasn't sure how, but the tears he'd been able to shed over John had struck him as a step in the right direction.

David's tired thoughts turned to Umbrella, to what role they'd played in Griffith's madness. While they surely hadn't meant for their researcher to go mad, they had created the circumstances that allowed it to happen; their complete disregard for human life could only have been encouragement for someone like Griffith. And without Umbrella, the scientist would never have had access to the T-Virus. . . .

Someday soon, they'll be held accountable for what they've done. Not today or tomorrow, but soon. . . .

Perhaps Trent would help them again. Perhaps Barry and Jill and Chris would uncover more in Raccoon. Perhaps—

Rebecca curled closer against him, her breath warm and even against his drying clothes, and David let the thoughts go for the time being, content to simply sit and not think at all. He was very, very tired.

As the first rays of the sun slipped over the horizon, Blake pronounced the waters clean, though neither David nor Rebecca heard him; both had fallen into a deep and dreamless sleep beneath the twilight of the coming day.

EPILOGUE

THE MEETING ROOM WAS A STUDY IN QUIET but unpretentious elegance. Three men sat at the stately oak table, a fourth standing by the window and staring out thoughtfully at the hazy morning sky. The man at the window could see the others reflected in the glass, though doubted that they noticed his careful scrutiny; for as sharp as they were politically, they tended to be fairly dull about watching what went on around them.

After the phone conference, the man who always wore blue spoke first, directly addressing the elderly man with the groomed mustache.

"Do we need to discuss the ramifications of this?" Blue asked.

Mustache sighed. "I believe the report covered them," he said airily.

The tea drinker broke in, setting his cup down with a

rattle. Steaming liquid slopped over the sides, distorting the tiny umbrella design that adorned the side.

"I don't think it's a wise idea to underestimate the magnitude of this . . . difficulty," Tea said. "Particularly not with the current *instability* factor in development. . . ."

Blue nodded. "I agree. Things like this have a way of getting out of hand. First the secondary in Raccoon, now the Cove—"

Mustache cut him off with a sharp glance. Blue, properly abashed, cleared his throat, his face red as he struggled to recover.

"That is to say, I believe there should be a more thorough investigation into these matters. Don't you think so, Mr. Trent?"

The man at the window turned around, wondering how these people had ever managed to get where they were. He didn't smile, knowing how much it bothered them when he didn't smile.

"I'm afraid I'll have to get back to you on that," Trent said coolly.

Blue nodded quickly. "Of course, take all the time you need. No hurry, gentlemen, am I right?"

Without another word, Trent turned and walked out of the room, outwardly as intimidating and precise as they expected him to be, as they *wanted* him to be.

Inside, he wondered how much longer the game could go on.

About the Author

S.D. (Stephani Danelle) Perry writes multimedia nov-
elizations in the fantasy/science-fiction/horror realm
for love and money, including several *Aliens* novels,
the novelization of *Timecop,* and the soon-to-be-
released movie thriller, *Virus.* Under the name Stella
Howard, she's written an original novel based upon
the television series *Xena, Warrior Princess.* The *Resident Evil* books mark her first foray into writing
novels based upon video games. She lives in Portland,
Oregon, with her husband and a multitude of pets.